Distracted

When Love Speaks

Contemporary Romance, Book One

ROBIN VAN AUKEN

Hands on Heritage LLC
589 Sylvan Dell Park Road
South Williamsport, PA 17701

DEDICATION

For Lance

WHEN LOVE SPEAKS

We are such stuff as dreams are made on,

and our little life is rounded with a sleep.

— William Shakespeare, The Tempest

CHAPTER ONE

Erin fidgeted in the pin-striped chair. The "two-minute" wait promised by the receptionist stretched into ten.

She glanced at the magazines spread on the side table. Shuffling through the pile, she found a new copy of "Them" magazine, a slick tabloid specializing in the latest scandals and love interests of the stars.

The headlines hyped the latest gossip about feuding politicians and love-struck actors. In the feature photo, a man and woman ducked their heads to avoid the paparazzi as they walked on a pier in a tropical locale. The man wore sunglasses, a pair of baggy shorts and sandals. Hmmm, nice abs, she thought.

The woman looked familiar. An actress, maybe? She wore a pink bikini with a black sarong knotted at her slim, tanned hip. Erin glanced out the large window at Washington's overcast skyline and shivered. Smog and low clouds obscured the Capitol dome. Spring and the Cherry Blossom Festival couldn't come soon enough.

She flipped through the magazine. Advertisements dominated the first ten pages, and then she came to the cover feature: The Island Couple. Most of the photos showed only the hunk. In one, he stood at the wheel of speed boat, shirtless, sunglasses on again, his dark wavy hair whipping in the wind. In another, he strummed a guitar at a beach bonfire.

"Like what you see?"

Erin dropped the magazine and stood.

"Patricia. How are you?"

"Fine. Have a seat, Erin."

Patricia McDowell slid behind her massive desk. An imperious veteran of the publishing trenches for more than thirty years, Patricia operated a company that churned out quality non-fiction. Her keen business sense resulted in books that dominated the top of the New York Times bestselling list.

Patricia valued Erin's efficiency, which paled in comparison to her charm and persistence. She discovered Erin succeeded in moving manuscripts through the system, from stalled authors' desks to the production department, more often through guile and wile, when experienced editors failed.

Erin's easy-going personality put many shy and introverted scholars at ease as she helped them complete their books on schedule.

Patricia couldn't care less if the girl recognized a split infinitive or a dangling participle. She employed plenty of grammarians. She wanted results and Erin delivered.

"Nice-looking man, isn't he?" Patricia lifted her chin towards the discarded tabloid.

"George Clooney? He's still yummy."

"No. The man on the cover."

"I didn't notice," Erin said. She picked up the magazine, thumbing through the pages until she found the beach photo spread again.

"He's okay, I guess. Who wouldn't be with that kind of money? How much do you think that speedboat cost?"

"I'm not sure, but the sailboat cost at least half a million. I know. I bought it for him."

"What? You're kidding me. You know this guy?" The magazine slipped through her fingers.

"That, my dear, is your next assignment. The boat was an advance on his forthcoming book."

Patricia smiled at Erin's disbelief. "Yes, he's that important, but he's a bit lackadaisical. He's missed several deadlines and his first chapter was due last month." Patricia leaned back into her leather chair and arched a silver eyebrow. "I cannot tolerate that. I need you on the project immediately."

"Is he local?" Erin picked up the magazine, flipped to the feature article and this time looked closer at the photographs.

"No. You'll have to travel for this one," Patricia said. Noting Erin's frown, she added, "He lives in North Carolina. Just a few hours away."

Erin chewed her lip. She preferred to work with professors, not playboys, especially those living near the Washington Beltway. She lived in Dupont Circle, near the fashionable northwest section of the city, but not as costly. Still, living in the capital was expensive and she could not afford to turn down a job.

"Can you leave right away?"

Erin fumbled through her jacket pocket and pulled out her mobile phone. Flipping through its digital calendar, she scanned the months of April and May. Nothing she couldn't reschedule.

"Yes. Do you have a dossier on this guy? What does he do?"

Patricia paused. "I'm sorry, no bio unless you count the 'Sexiest Man in America' feature in 'Them.' He's an artist and you won't believe what they're paying for his paintings. Your job is to make sure he finishes this book. Hell, I need you to make sure he begins it. I envision a book that can be used in a university setting by art students, and still entertain the layperson. He's an exciting talent. It's imperative we publish the book while he's still on top. An illustrated autobiography by Stephen Spence will sell very well."

"What's his name? Stephen Spence?" Erin echoed.

"Have you heard of him?"

"I'm not sure. I'll have to do some research. I guess these magazines are the best place to begin," Erin said, dropping the tabloid on the table. "The paparazzi like to follow him. Who are the women?"

"Who knows? He's seldom seen with the same one twice. He doesn't appear to be lonely, does he?"

Erin heaved a sigh. "Men like him seldom are."

* * *

Not sure how long the project would last, Erin over packed. She decided to keep her appearance professional and maintain a dressy-casual style for work. To her traditional "librarian garb," she added a new cocktail dress. She also packed cotton tops and shorts since spring came earlier in the Carolinas. Stephen Spence lived by the Atlantic Ocean, so she could beach comb, maybe swim during her free time. She tossed an assortment of undergarments, and her bathing suit into the mix. Next, she went through the medicine cabinet and the shower, dumping products into a water-proof tote.

Aidan leaned against the bathroom door, eating a protein bar. "Hey, what's going on?"

Erin's ex-husband, Aidan Carter, was a full-time university student, working on his Ph.D. Their marriage ended when she discovered his love affair with another student.

During the year it took for their divorce to finalize, her rage and anguish at his betrayal faded. Erin allowed him back into her life, but as her childhood friend, not a husband.

Erin agreed to be roommates, at least while Aidan finished his doctoral degree. A poor college student, he couldn't afford his own apartment in D.C., so he used the spare bedroom. He paid rent, when he could, and bartered cleaning and cooking services when he couldn't.

Sometimes, though, Aidan forgot they were "roommates" and poked his nose into her business.

"I have an assignment. I'll be gone for at least a month, I imagine," Erin said.

"What's the assignment?"

"I'm going to North Carolina. Patricia has a client who can't meet his deadlines. I have to go down there and crack the whip."

"Who is this client and how old is he?"

"Jealous?" she asked.

"Maybe," he said.

"Well, don't be. It's work," Erin said, relieved she hadn't brought home the magazine with photos of Stephen Spence. "Besides, you have your life and I have mine. Remember?"

"I remember, but I care about you," he said. Then he glanced into her suitcase and noticed the mass of frilly underwear and the bathing suit.

"Looks more like a vacation to me," he said, a frown creasing his forehead.

Erin closed her suitcase and zipped the flap, suppressing a grin. What would Aidan say about her spending the next month at the beach with a handsome and rich playboy?

"Well, it's not."

CHAPTER TWO

Erin drove the twelve hours to Hatteras in a short-lease SUV. Living in a major city with a Metro system, she didn't need a car. With McDowell Publishing picking up the rental car tab, she opted for something large and safe.

She rolled into the ferry parking lot at Swan Quarter at twilight.

"Great. That's just great," she muttered, climbing out of the vehicle and walking to the pier. A weather beaten "Closed" sign swung on a chain strung across the entrance. The last ferry to the island faded to a speck in the distance.

Back at the SUV, Erin turned on the overhead light and studied the GPS, flipping through the digital maps. There was no feasible way to drive to the island. She would have to stay on the mainland and catch the morning ferry.

She backtracked to Route 264 and checked into a small roadside motel. In the lobby, she found a shelf with colorful brochures. She shuffled through them until she found one with the ferry schedule, then tucked it into her purse while the desk clerk ran her credit card.

"Is there a restaurant close by?"

The clerk, a somber, dark-skinned man, shook his head. "There is a convenience store across the street," he suggested.

Instead, Erin stopped at the vending machines near the staircase and punched the buttons for a bottle of water and a pack of peanut butter crackers. She fed more dollar bills into the machine, and then selected a bag of chips and a chocolate bar.

An hour later, showered and wrapped in her fleece robe, she sat cross-legged on the littered motel bed, surrounded by junk food wrappers and cracker crumbs. With the remote control in one hand and a candy bar in the other, she flipped through the channels, searching for a weather update. The old television brought in local news only, and none of them included a forecast. Her cell phone trilled, and she dove for her purse. She scanned the caller ID before pushing the green answer button.

"Aidan?"

"Hi. How was the drive?"

Erin chewed her lower lip. "Okay."

"Did you make good time?"

"Aidan. You don't have to check on me."

"I'm not."

"Yes, you are."

After several silent seconds, Erin continued, "I'm not going to talk about this again," Erin said. "You've got things to do. I've got things to do. I can't have you calling me every night."

"Fine. Good night." He ended the call.

Erin shook her head at his abrupt farewell, turned off her phone and tossed it on the side table. She swung her legs off the bed and snatched her tote bag from suitcase, tossing it on the bathroom counter. At sink, she brushed her teeth with vigor and flossed until her gums bled. She twisted her long, blonde hair, tying it into a loose knot, then leaned towards the glass and glared at her reflection. "Men!"

Before turning off the light, she programmed her cell phone to send all calls from Aidan to voice mail.

* * *

In the morning, Erin placed three outfits on the bed and stepped back. The first was a skirt and jacket she found at a boutique known for its expensive haute couture clothing. A "power suit," it exuded sexiness. The soft gray blouse with plunging neck line complemented the pencil skirt and black, patent-leather pumps.

The second outfit consisted of a sleeveless, blue sweater and a pair of flare-legged khakis. The pants emphasized her slim waist and curvy hips. The sweater showed her trim, strong arms to an advantage. A pair of brown boots with a side zipper finished the ensemble.

She considered the third outfit, a pair of light-weight shorts and a cotton T-shirt combined with a pair of hiking sandals. The outfit was modest and comfortable and less intimidating than the first two choices. Considering the photographs she'd seen of Spence, she decided on a low-key approach and opted for the shorts.

She still hadn't been able to find a weather forecast on the television, so she peeked between the heavy, vinyl drapes. A blanket of fog obscured her view. She could see the front bumper of her rental SUV, which may or may not have been the only car in the parking lot. She shivered, then went back to her suitcase and pulled out a zippered hoodie.

Twenty minutes later, after a hasty stop for a continental breakfast in the hotel lobby, Erin drove back to the Swan Quarter ferry with time to spare. She sat in the SUV after paying for a ticket and waited for the "Governor Hyde" to begin loading. At 160-feet long, the Sound Class ferry carried thirty-five vehicles. Her car was third in line and twenty cars followed.

Soon, her turn came to board and she drove up the

creaking, steel ramp. An old man wearing a Greek fisherman's cap stood in front of the SUV. He coaxed her forward with a gloved hand. When her bumper was inches from the car in front, the man signaled halt, then gave her a quick thumbs up. She shifted into park, turned the engine off and set the parking brake as instructed.

She ignored the cold, damp wind, pulled her hoodie on and climbed out of the truck. The dull yellow disc of the rising sun grew brighter over the bow of the boat as it plowed eastward through a light chop. She leaned over the rail, settled a pair of sunglasses on her nose and watched as seagulls circled around the ferry. In the distance, as visibility improved, she spied a sailboat. The morning fog burned away and the noisy ship chugged through the Pamlico Sound.

* * *

More than two hours later, the ferry landed at Ocracoke. First car on the ship meant last one off, so Erin disembarked after most of the other drivers. She parked in a lonely corner of the lot, then programmed the GPS receiver with Spence's address. She studied the network of roads until she located his house. The mechanical voice of the GPS commanded: "Head south on Northpoint toward Pamlico Shores Road."

Erin smiled. During the past two days, she'd grown accustomed to the disembodied female voice and nicknamed her "Becky." She put the SUV into gear and drove out of the ferry lot towards the small village of Ocracoke.

"Turn left at Pamlico Shores Road and drive point-one miles before turning right at British Cemetery Road," Becky ordered.

"And we're on our way," Erin chimed.

She drove the small paved road to the stop sign and looked right. The shimmering Pamlico Sound lay beyond a beach house at the curve. To the left, she saw scrubby shrubs, twisted cypress trees and the roof tops of island cottages. The roadway was narrow with no markings and no other cars were in sight.

She drove on.

"In 500 feet, turn left onto Back Road," Becky piped.

As she drove, Erin saw a small, rundown cottage with folding chairs stacked on the porch. An oak tree's limbs stretched over the structure, shading it and inhibiting grass from taking root. A rusted blue truck and a trailer hauling a white bass boat were parked in the driveway. A hand-lettered sign propped against the mailbox offered night crawlers and cut bait.

"Hmmm... Spence's neighbors aren't that fashionable."

On the left, she noticed a small burial ground bordered by a weather-beaten wood fence.

"Hence the name 'Cemetery Road,'" Erin said aloud, having started to converse with Becky the previous afternoon.

She stopped the car in the middle of the road and looked at the headstones. Most were small, old markers, discolored with black and green mildew. Stunted, windswept trees bordered the back of the cemetery.

She drove on, passing more houses. "The neighborhood's improving," she told Becky.

She braked to a crawl and turned onto Back Road. On her right, an odd-shaped, cedar-sheathed house contrasted with its neighbor, an elegant, older home with white-washed siding and a large wrap-around porch. Because of rising seawater during tropical storms and hurricanes, many of the island's buildings sat high on pilings.

"Continue point four miles, then turn left at State Road 1341," Becky's monotone continued.

As Erin drove, the scenery contained more of the same. She passed unmarked roads bounded by rustic cottages, shrubs, sawgrass, palmettos and stunted oak trees.

"Drive point three miles, then turn left onto road."

"No name, eh?" Erin squinted into the sun as she searched for her turn.

"Satellite signal lost," Becky announced. The cartoon car on the GPS screen became a question mark.

"Thanks a lot, Becky." Erin slowed even more after checking the rear-view mirror and seeing nobody on the road. She had to be close. In the distance, she saw luxurious houses. They were tall, wood and glass sentinels amid the saw grass. They all faced Pamlico Sound.

"Ahhh, here's the money," Erin noted.

She passed two unmarked, black-topped roads and decided to keep looking. Ahead, on the left, she saw a battered mailbox next to a narrow, unpaved road. She imagined the entrance to the playboy's property would be grand, like the lavish houses she'd seen earlier. The rusting mailbox, impaled by an unpainted wooden post and set in a five-gallon bucket filled with concrete, could not belong to a famous artist, she thought.

"Probably not the road I want to take, right Becky?" she asked the GPS receiver. No answer, of course. Becky's screen only showed the question mark. "Afraid to commit, are we?"

Erin pressed the button to lower the window and leaned out for a better look at the address on the box. Faded stick-on letters read: "S_ence."

"You would think a guy like that could afford a decent mailbox," she said. After checking the mirrors for oncoming traffic, she backed up several yards, then turned onto the sand and gravel trail.

As Erin drove, she admired the topography as it changed from swampy to open, sandy space.

"Arriving at destination on left," Becky chimed, having regained her bearings.

Erin stopped in front of a large gray house. It floated on brick pilings in a field of sea grass. Unpainted, the wood-shingled house featured a gabled roof and long engaged dormers. Hinged, wood-batten shutters were held open with a stick, protecting the old-fashioned sash windows. A wrap-around porch encircled the house and behind it, she glimpsed a long stretch of white beach and blue water.

She didn't see a driveway, so she stopped her truck close to the edge of the road. She checked her watch. It was after noon and, according to Patricia, Mr. Spence expected her. In fact, he suggested she stay at his house during her visit to the island. She hiked the fifty yards to the front door, wading through sea oats and saw grass that whipped and scratched her bare legs.

She hissed, then licked a finger and rubbed it on a long, bloody scratch. "I should have worn pants."

After plucking sticker burrs from her shorts and shaking sand from her shoes, Erin mounted the steps and pressed the doorbell. She waited a minute or two before pressing it again. After several minutes, she tried knocking on the door. There was no answer.

She frowned. He knew she arrived today, so he wouldn't have left town, she reasoned. After peeking in the windows and detecting no signs of life, she knocked harder, calling, "Mr. Spence. Hello. Mr. Spence?"

Looking for another entrance, Erin walked around the side porch but a locked screen door barred access. She retraced her steps to the front, went down the stairs and around the porch. Past the screen door, the land sloped downward. With no stairs in sight, she decided to wiggle through the railing. She tossed her handbag first. Then, using the railing as a ladder she scrambled up and slithered onto the porch.

She leaned against a column and studied her surroundings. A few feet away, a man lay in a cord-twisted hammock. He wore faded, ragged shorts and sunglasses. A pair of flip flops and three empty beer bottles on the deck completed the vignette.

Now, the mailbox seems appropriate, Erin thought.

She stood, brushed sand off her shorts and walked towards the sleeping man. She hesitated waking him and instead, spent several heartbeats assessing him. His wavy sun-streaked hair was a bit long and unkempt. He had a broad forehead and a wide mouth. He kept in shape, she noted. His arms were large and well-muscled. He had a spare tire, however, so if this was Mr. Spence, he had forgone the crunches. A thatch of copper hair traced his chest, snaking into the waistband of his faded Bermuda shorts. His feet were long and his large toes splayed. He must not wear shoes often, she thought.

"Do I know you?"

His slow, Southern drawl caught her by surprise. She thought he'd been sleeping. Playing opossum instead. She took a step back.

"Mr. Spence? I'm Erin Andersen. I've been sent by Patricia McDowell to help you with your book."

He lifted his sunglasses. Steel blue eyes squinted.

"Hey, move over here, would ya? Can't see who I'm talkin' to."

Erin picked up her purse and moved to the far side of the hammock, the late-morning sun shining on her face. Spence took in her sandals, her legs, shorts and shirt. He stared at her chest before moving to her face. Then he grinned. His teeth were bright white against tanned skin.

"Well, howdy. I forgot you were coming. You want a beer?"

Erin hesitated, then decided she needed to make friends fast.

"Sure. It's been a long, thirsty trip," she lied.

Stephen Spence gestured at a bar against the back of the house and said, "Me too. Why don't you grab us a couple. What'd you say your name was?"

He hadn't moved out of the hammock. He pointed a finger towards an outdoor kitchen and dropped his sunglasses back into place. Erin dropped her purse on the deck and walked to the bar. Behind it, she discovered a sink, several drawers and a small, built-in refrigerator. Inside were at least three dozen Coronas, so cold they formed ice crystals when she pulled out two bottles.

"Opener's on the counter there. Limes, too."

She picked up the ancient and rusty bottle opener. Glad I've had a tetanus shot, she thought. A basket of limes sat on the counter next to a plastic cutting board. Recalling college days with tequila shots and lemons, she rolled the lime, softening its rind so the juice flowed. She pulled open a couple of drawers until she found a sharp knife, then sliced the fruit. She tucked the lime into the long necks and the beer fizzed. She walked over to Spence and handed him one. The other, she upended, amazed at how good it tasted.

"Ahh, be still my heart," he said and drained half the bottle.

Fascinated, Erin watched as he licked the lime from his lips and smiled at her.

Well, I'm off on the right foot, she thought. She searched for a chair and not finding one, headed back to the bar, brushed off stray crumbs and hoisted herself onto the counter. Obviously, this was a one-person deck and guests had to make do. If he wasn't going to provide a chair, she'd find her own seat.

"You know, sometimes that's my kitchen table."

"I don't mind. These are old shorts," she lied again. She lifted the bottle to her lips. Another shot of courage, she thought.

He chuckled, a low rumble. "You're kind of feisty, aren't you?"

"No, Mr. Spence. I'm here to do whatever it takes to help you write your book."

She waited. She learned that sometimes, in situations where the client didn't appreciate professional intervention, reaction worked better than proaction. She bided her time.

Unfortunately, Stephen Spence didn't mind waiting. He

rocked the hammock, pushing it with one large foot planted on the deck.

Erin capitulated. "Do you have any questions?"

"Nope."

He upended the beer, savoring the last of it. He shook the bottle at her expressively, then put it on the deck by the other three empties.

Erin exhaled, blowing wayward tendrils off her forehead. She lifted her bottle and drank it in a series of chugs, then licked the lime pulp off her lips. After setting her bottle to the side, she jumped off the bar and once again bent to open the fridge. Out of the corner of her eye, she saw him lift his sunglasses.

"Are you checking me out?"

"Yes ma'am. You sure have nice legs."

Erin shuffled her feet to the left, giving him a profile of her rear instead of a full-on view. "Perv," she muttered. She pulled two more beers from the ice box and slid lime slices into bottles. She walked to the hammock and put the icy beer into his hand. She lifted her long neck bottle in salute and took a deep pull before hopping back up on the bar.

"I'm told you're having problems meeting your deadlines."

He didn't reply as he rocked in the hammock, the cold beer cradled in his right hand.

"You do understand why I'm here, don't you Mr. Spence?"

"Spence."

Erin felt a flash of impatience. "You do understand why I'm here, don't you?"

"Yep."

She pulled a small notebook from her short's pocket and clicked her ink pen, the tip poised over a fresh sheet of paper. "I think the first thing we should do is make a schedule."

Spence snorted and raised his beer to his lips.

"You think that's funny?"

He lifted his sunglasses and winked at her. "Honey, I don't have a schedule."

"Well, now you do, Mr. Spence. You've signed a contract to produce a book, and there are deadlines to meet. I'm here to make sure you do. And," she added, "I'm not your 'honey.'"

"Touchy, eh? You married?"

"No. Not that it's any of your business," Erin said, her face impassive as she stared across the wetlands.

"Relax, sweetheart. Just don't want some angry husband knocking on the door next week."

"Well, you won't. And don't call me sweetheart, either."

"Don't you like men?"

Erin sputtered angrily. This conversation is getting way out of control, she thought. "Mr. Spence ..."

"Spence."

"Mr. Spence! I'm here to do a job. My sexual preferences are none of your concern."

"So hands off, huh?"

"If I want a relationship, I'll get a puppy," she snarled.

"Hmmm. Sounds like the voice of experience," Spence observed.

Erin frowned. In the distance, the Pamlico Sound shimmered.

* * *

Four beers later Erin was sitting on the deck, her legs stretched in front of her, burning in the mid-afternoon sun. She felt loopy. Her continental breakfast consisted of a plain bagel and a Styrofoam cup of bitter orange juice. She missed dinner the night before. She began chewing on lime rinds and peeking into the cracks of the deck for stray peanuts.

So far she'd learned that Stephen Spence never woke

before noon, and it was only because he fell asleep in the hammock late last night that she had the pleasure of his company now.

He also talked a bit about Ocracoke, telling her how his family came to the small island.

"I was born here. There's not many of us, only about 800 or so year-round residents. My folks came to the Outer Banks in the '60s and opened one of the first dive shops in the area. My dad was in the Navy and learned how to dive. He taught my mom, and they worked together for years."

Erin liked listening to his soft, Southern accent. "How long have they been married?"

"My dad is gone now. He died a few years ago."

"Oh, sorry to hear that."

Spence sobered. "He died of emphysema. He smoked."

"What about your mom? How is she?"

"She gets along. Still runs the dive shop. She's a tough old bird."

"How old is she?"

"Well, I'm the youngest, and she had me late. She was in her forties, I think. Surprised when I came along. She's in her seventies now, but she doesn't act like it."

Finally, he swung his legs out of the hammock and walked over to his guest. She licked her lips. They felt swollen and more hairy than the kneecaps in front of her. He offered his hand and she put her left one into his and waited.

"One, two, three."

He pulled her to her feet at "three" and smiled. Devastating, she thought, her gut clenching at his brilliant, white smile.

She leaned against the bar and burped.

"Oh, my gosh! Excuse me," she said. "I'm not used to drinking beer for lunch." She valiantly swallowed the next burp.

"Don't apologize. I'm impressed." Spence smiled again,

disarming her. "Let's go inside. You've had too much sun."

He picked up her bag and slung it over his shoulder. Then he put a hand on her back and steered her towards a sliding glass door. Inside, her head began to clear. It was at least twenty degrees cooler and she spied a large sofa.

"Sanctuary!"

"I take it you're not from the South?"

Uninhibited by the alcohol, Erin slumped on the couch, then sighed.

"No. I'm from Pennsylvania."

"You tired?"

"Mmm hmm."

"How 'bout you take a nap while I shower? You mind if I leave you alone for a while?"

Erin snored softly.

"I'll take that as a yes."

Honey blonde hair spilled out of a ponytail and covered her face. He was tempted to brush it back.

* * *

Twenty minutes later, Erin woke and realized she had to pee. She sat and felt woozy. Whoa, she thought, what have I done? No matter; her bladder was more important. She walked down the hall and opened every door. She found the bathroom on the fourth try. She pulled her shorts down and sat on the toilet. Relief was immediate. She put her elbows on her knees and rubbed her eyes.

"Could you hand me that towel?"

Her head snapped up and she looked towards the shower. Stephen Spence, half hidden behind a fogged glass door, turned off the water and noticed his guest had found him once more.

She dropped her head in her hands and muttered, "Why me?" then tugged the towel off the bar and proffered it in his direction.

"Thanks. 'Preciate that."

He closed the shower door and turned away, whistling "How Much Is That Doggie in the Window?"

Erin peeked through her fingers and watched through the foggy glass as he dried off with the towel, his back to her. Despite her best intentions, she let her eyes slide down, taking in the wet curls against his neck, the broad expanse of his back tapering into a slim waist. Seconds later, she slipped through the door but not before stealing one last peek at the man in the shower. He finished drying off and wrapped the towel low around his waist. As he stepped out of the shower, she closed the door and sprinted towards the living room.

Spence didn't bother dressing. He followed her into the living room and collapsed into one of the large armchairs. He exhaled loudly. "That's a chore. You ever notice that taking a shower is a lot like work?"

Erin looked away.

"No. I, um, generally take showers early. I find it refreshing."

"That so? I don't generally get up early."

Erin laughed. Embarrassed, she attempted to act and converse normally, though she still looked away. "Mr. Spence, I apologize. I didn't mean to intrude. I had to use the bathroom and didn't realize you were there also."

"Call me Spence."

"I don't think I've gotten off on the right foot here. I ..." Erin trailed off. She stared out the sliding glass doors at the back bay and licked her swollen lips. "If you want me to leave, I understand. I'm sure I can find a motel on the island."

"Are you thirsty?"

"What?"

"Are you thirsty? You keep licking your lips like you're thirsty."

She bit her lower lip, confirming the fact that they were still there although she still couldn't feel them. Alcohol did that to her. "I am. I need some water."

He stood up, retied his towel, and walked into the kitchen. Now she was the one looking.

Erin heard ice clinking, followed by a stream of water. He brought her the glass and as she reached for it, he sat next to her. She downed it in several large gulps. He watched as her throat jiggled. She lifted the glass to her forehead and closed her eyes.

"It's so hot here. It feels like summer already."

Smiling, Spence took the glass from her.

"Why don't you lie down and relax. You got a little burned out there. You may have sun stroke."

"Really? Is that serious?"

"Can be. Some people die from it. You're probably just dehydrated."

Erin's head swam. She closed her eyes and sank into the cool sofa cushions. Spence stood and after placing a pillow under her head, went into his bedroom to dress.

* * *

Hours later, Erin woke up. She felt lost. She blinked to clear her vision and heard music in the distance. She followed it down the hallway and found Spence in his studio, standing at a large canvas.

He frowned as he concentrated, then glanced back and forth from the painting to several photographs he had clipped to the corner of the easel. A tackle box filled with paint tubes sat on a tall table next to his hip. He'd removed the tackle box tray and used it as a palette. The table top also worked as a palette. Layers of dried paint stacked one on top of another like an artistic archaeological dig. He had a brush behind one ear and chewed on another. He didn't move for several minutes, studying the scene before him. He didn't notice Erin, her footsteps muffled by the carpet.

He glanced first over his shoulder at the sun now

sinking into the Pamlico Sound then back at his canvas before he spied her. She didn't move.

"The light's wrong now," he said as he put the brushes in a bottle of linseed oil. He dropped the tray onto the table behind him, then sauntered towards her. "How ya feeling?"

"Fine. I think I'll find a motel on the island and freshen up."

"I thought you were going to stay here."

Erin backed away as he approached the door. "I think you and I need a bit of privacy and maybe a fresh start." Even as the words came out, she realized they did not sound convincing.

"Nah, no worries. I've already put your suitcase in your room. It's at the end of the hall," he said, dropping a hand on her shoulder and escorting her to the opposite side of the house. He opened a door, dazzling Erin with the view from the large windows. The room floated in light as the mirrored closets on the far wall reflected the blues and browns of the wetlands. A king-sized bed covered with a champagne silk spread dominated the center of the room. He moved to one of the mirrored doors and opened it.

"See? Your own bathroom." He emphasized the word "own."

Erin cringed, but the recollection of his wet body flushed her cheeks, not his gentle teasing.

"I unpacked for ya," he added, stepping towards the built-in dresser and opening the top drawer. He pulled out a lacy bra and swung it around his index finger.

She gasped. He'd retrieved her suitcase from the SUV while she slept and put her clothes away? He dropped the bra, closed the drawer and changed the subject.

"Hungry?"

"Yes," she replied, disarmed by the simple question.

"I don't have much in the way of vittles here, so we'll go out. I suppose you'll want to take a shower? You might want to lock the door. You know, to keep out intruders."

He stifled a laugh, backed out of the room and closed the door.

Erin rolled her eyes at his jibe. Functioning on auto pilot, she stepped into the bathroom, a replica of the one she barged into earlier. Spence placed her toiletries on the counter and her shampoo and conditioner in the shower. She opened the mirrored medicine cabinet and found her toothbrush, her floss, and other toiletries.

She stepped out of the bathroom and into the walk-in closet. Pulling open drawers she found her lingerie, stockings, shorts and shirts. Her dresses hung on satin-padded hangers. He left out the red cocktail dress, her new favorite with its cut-away back and short tulle skirt. He'd arranged her silver slingback sandals with their four-inch heels, beside the dress.

Obviously, he expected her to wear it tonight.

Erin sat on the bed and fumed at the invasion of her privacy. It was obvious, he didn't respect boundaries. She considered calling Patricia and dropping the project. But, in truth, she invaded his space when she climbed onto the deck. And she'd invaded his privacy when she barged into his bathroom.

Instead of complaining to Patricia, she went into the bathroom and turned on the shower. She'd handled tougher clients than Stephen Spence and she refused to let him under her skin. A lazy womanizer was no match for an organized, professional editor.

"It's on," she said to her reflection, then she dressed for battle.

Erin's red skirt flared above her knees in baby-doll fashion. The silver high heels made her short legs appear long. They were sunburned from her morning on the deck, so she decided not to wear stockings. She slathered her skin with fragrant lotion, and applied makeup, since the dress called for a bit of war paint.

The casual, tomboy approach hadn't worked. Sharing a few beers on the deck had been a bad idea. The man needed to take her seriously.

Sleek and polished, she stepped into the living room, her small evening bag in her hand. Spence, sitting in an armchair and toying with the TV remote, whistled.

"I didn't think you'd wear it," he said, referring to her dress.

"Why not? That's why I brought it."

Her icy voice sent shivers down his spine. "You clean up nice," he said.

Erin sashayed into the center of the room and batted her lashes. "Thank you. Wish I could say the same."

It was another lie. Spence wore a pair of tan, baggy pants, a black silk shirt and leather boat shoes. He'd brushed back his wavy dark hair but hadn't bothered to shave. He looked reckless and sexy.

He placed a hand over his heart and tossed his head back, laughing. "Now that's just unkind." He walked towards Erin. "What can I do to improve your opinion of me?"

"Obey me. We've got a lot of work ahead of us."

Spence bowed. "As you wish."

She smiled and turned towards what she hoped was the front door. They didn't speak as they walked outside. Without a word, Spence whisked her into his arms and waded through the tall grass towards her SUV.

Erin gasped at the touch of his warm hand cupping her bare legs while the other snaked around her back and curved under her arm. His fingertips brushed the side of her breast.

"Hey! Put me down."

"Quit complaining," Spence said. "You'd never make it through the yard in those shoes."

Erin flinched as his warm breath caressed her cheek. She closed her eyes and clutched her purse tight.

Seconds later, Spence set her on her feet at the passenger door and held out his hand. He knew the town best, she reasoned, handing him the keys and waiting while he opened the door. He watched as she maneuvered into the high vehicle, tuck her short skirt under her thigh, and then he closed the door. He slid behind the wheel, started the truck and headed towards town.

Ten minutes later, Spence parked at a local restaurant, the tires crunching on the crushed shell lot. "You like seafood?"

"No," she said sniffing at the tantalizing aroma of grilling meat. "But I do like steak."

She didn't wait for him to open her door. Instead, she slid carefully, placing one high heel on the running board while the other floated inches from the ground.

"You need help?" Spence asked, keeping his eyes on her thighs as her dress rode high.

"No thank you. I'm fine," she said as she dropped, groping for the door handle.

"Yes you are," he agreed.

CHAPTER THREE

Spence poured Erin another glass of wine. "You know, that is fascinating," he said.

She monopolized the conversation during dinner with her detailed explanation of book outlines and the importance of schedules.

"Really? You think so?"

"No. I'm saying that so you'll drink more."

Erin steeled herself against his smile, his Southern drawl, and the spreading warmth of the red wine. She finished her steak and salad, and progressed to slathering butter on thick slices of brown bread.

Spence cracked open crab legs, mounding the pink and white meat on the plate. He speared the crab meat with a tiny fork, dipping it in one of several containers of drawn butter in front of him, before savoring each bite. Erin swore he'd been eating for an hour.

"Can't you go any faster?"

"You can help, you know," he said, offering her the pliers.

"Ewww. No."

"Why don't you like seafood?" he asked, sucking on a cracked leg.

"It all tastes the same to me. Gross."

"You should try this. It's not gross." Spence offered her a minuscule forkful of white crabmeat, dripping with butter.

"No, I don't like it." She stuffed a piece of bread into her mouth. "Besides, I'm full."

Spence eyed her puffed cheeks, then tilted his head, a faraway look in his eyes. "Do you hear that?"

"What?" Erin listened for sirens. Life in the city numbed her to loud noises.

"They're playing our song." He wiped his hands on a napkin, stood and pulled her to her feet. They glided toward the empty terrace and swayed in the dark, his free arm around her waist.

"I don't hear anything," she said, putting a hand on his chest and pushing away.

"Listen," he whispered. He lifted her hand to his shoulder, then pulled her close and danced. Below, in the restaurant's kitchen, a radio played a reggae tune.

She stepped out of his embrace and put her hands on her hips. "You realize, this is not a date."

Spence shrugged, then leaned over the terrace rail and looked at the boats moored in Silver Lake Harbor. "Over there is Anchorage Marina. That's where my mom runs the dive shop. That's where I keep my boats."

"Boats? You have more than one?" Erin asked, approaching the rail and peering into the dark.

"I've got a few. You'll like them."

"I'm sure I will," Erin said. "I've seen photographs of them. Fancy yachts filled with beautiful women."

He grinned. "I wouldn't call them yachts. I've got a sport fisher and a sailboat. I've also got a small Boston whaler. Nothing fancy. They're work boats."

"Work boats?"

"Sure. I do a lot of exploring when I'm considering what to paint. I work from photographs I take in the wild."

"Right. What about all of the beautiful women?"

"All women are beautiful to me, darlin'."

"I'm not your 'darlin'."

Spence studied Erin's face, assessing her green eyes, sooty lashes and honey blonde hair. Soft, full lips crowned a dimpled chin. She tried to hide a smirk and it dimpled her cheek. But it was the determined look that narrowed her eyes, the stubborn tilt of her chin, that he found most attractive.

"I'd say you're the most beautiful woman I've ever met," he said, stretching out a seductive hand to caress her cheek.

She wasn't buying it. She snorted and arched away from his questing finger tips. "Hah! You'd say it, but it's not true and you know it. I'm calling B.S."

* * *

After dinner, they strolled on the beach. Spence tucked Erin's tiny purse into his back pocket and carried her shoes by their straps. Even in the moonlight, she spotted shells and gathered them by the handfuls, collecting them in her skirt.

"Tomorrow you'll just toss those out," he predicted.

"No, I won't. They're beautiful."

"Happens all the time. People pick up seashells and then toss them away the next day because they're not perfect. They start discriminating because one is chipped, or they find a prettier one."

Erin considered his logic, then released the edges of her skirt. The shells tumbled to the beach.

"Tell me about your sailboat," she commanded, brushing the sand from her hands.

"It's a 50-foot catamaran. It's got a saloon, a full galley, a master suite and two double berths, each with their own heads. Sorry. I know you like to use my bathroom."

Erin rolled her eyes. "Let it go," she warned.

ROBIN VAN AUKEN

"The cockpit is large and it has a dive platform on the back. Do you dive?"

"No, I'm a freshwater girl. I grew up near a big lake in Pennsylvania."

"Oh yeah? Where about?"

"Eaton. It's a small town in the mountains, hours from anywhere."

"Your family still live there?"

"Yes, my sister and her husband still live in the family home. My parents are retired and live in Florida."

"Just you and your sister?"

"That's right, just us. I barely know my cousins. My parents seldom left the farm to visit family. We had livestock that needed constant care. Instead of vacations, we kept a cabin down by the lake."

"You a farm girl?"

"Used to be. I'm a city girl now. I have an apartment in D.C. Have you been there?"

"Sure, I like the way they've improved the waterfront there. They have a nice boardwalk and a few good patio bars."

"Boats and bars. Why am I not surprised?"

Spence smiled and took one of her free hands, wiping the sand on his shirt before clasping it in his. Erin tugged her hand from his.

"I'm a big girl. I don't need you to hold my hand."

They retraced their footprints along the shore to the parking lot, retrieved the SUV, and drove back to Spence's house in silence.

He turned at the battered black mailbox that Erin missed earlier in the day.

"What's the deal with the trashy mailbox?"

"It helps keep the riffraff out, along with the models from all the photo shoots," he said.

"Very funny. I bet every one of them ended ... at your house." She almost said, "in your bed."

Spence smiled, drove down a private driveway and

28

parked the SUV beside the house.

"How did I miss this?" Erin abandoned the vehicle on the side of the road that afternoon, not noticing the discreet parking area.

"You were supposed to. That's how I designed the property."

At the front door, he lifted a hidden panel and pushed buttons. The door opened, low lights turned on and soft music began to play.

"Wow, Double-Oh-Seven, you've got quite a place."

He smirked and stood aside, letting her enter first.

"My feet are sandy," she warned. Spence shrugged.

She dropped her shoes by the front door along with her small purse and walked into the living room.

"Well, thanks for an exciting first day, Mr. Spence. I'll see you tomorrow morning." She headed for her room, but he caught her wrist.

"You shouldn't go to bed yet. You should drink some water. Don't want to wake up with a hangover."

He maneuvered her into the kitchen and pulled a couple bottles of cold spring water from the refrigerator. Then, he opened the sliding glass doors to the patio and ushered her into the night air.

"Let's watch the stars," he suggested. He sat sideways in the hammock, his feet planted on the deck, then patted the netting next to him. Once again, Erin sought alternative seating. Her choices were the bar or the deck or the hammock.

"Okay. Move over."

They rocked for several minutes gazing at the stars. She tried not to focus on his arm and leg, warm against her. She relaxed, but still felt a little chilled from her sunburn. When she shivered, Spence asked, "You cold?" He lifted his arm, crossing it behind his head, and she rolled into the curve against him.

"A little." Erin allowed herself to huddle closer, absorbing his body heat and inhaling his clean, fresh scent.

Her arms and legs felt heavy. It was too easy to close her eyes and sigh.

"I used to lie in the hammock with my daddy when I was a child. Down at the cabin near our house. We spent a lot of our summers out there at the lake."

She yawned. After several minutes of quiet rocking, Erin slept.

CHAPTER FOUR

"Wake up, sleepy head."

Erin opened her eyes to a dusky blue dawn. She tried to sit but the sudden movement rocked the hammock and it started to flip over.

"Whoa." Spence put anchoring foot on the deck and caught her about the waist before she tumbled out.

"Did we sleep out here?" Erin's strapless dress bunched around her waist and sand still clung to the skirt. Thank goodness, she thought, her top was still in place.

"I'm a mess." She ran her tongue over her teeth and smacked he lips. "I need my toothbrush."

Spence smiled at her lack of pretension and her tousled hair.

"And you've got bed head," he added.

"Well, you're not so pretty yourself this morning."

Actually, he was.

"I'm not supposed to be," he said.

"And I am? That's a chauvinistic thing to say."

"I didn't say it."

"You intimated it. Never mind, I've got to pee."

"Want me to come along?"

"Thanks; I can handle this one alone."

She stood and gave the hammock a shove. Her fingers still wrapped in the webbing, she jerked it back and tumbled Spence onto the deck.

"I'll remember this."

Erin stuck out her tongue, then scooted through the sliding doors and down the hallway and into her room. She tossed her crumpled dress on the floor and turned on the shower. She washed her hair and poured a generous helping of gel on the puff. As she scrubbed her body she ran her hands down her arms. Hugging herself, she thought about Spence's smile.

"Don't do this," she said aloud. "This is not a vacation. He is your client. No hanky panky allowed."

She opted for shorts and a white T-shirt. She didn't bother drying her hair and instead of using makeup, she applied a moisturizer. She surveyed herself in the mirror. No more sexy, she avowed. From now on, it's plain old Erin.

She went in search of food and found a pot of coffee brewing on the kitchen counter. She pulled open drawers and cabinet doors until she found a cup and a spoon. Thank goodness, she thought, as she located a pint of half-and-half in the refrigerator. Now where does he keep the sugar? She found it, and not much more, behind a sliding panel. He was right; he didn't have many "vittles" in his pantry.

She took the steaming mug to the living room and curled on the couch. She enjoyed quiet, relaxing mornings. Then she heard the distinct ring of her cell phone. She spotted the evening bag by the front door. She put the coffee mug on the side table and went to answer the call.

"Erin? Where are you? Have you met with Mr. Spence?"

"Patricia? Hi. Yes, I have."

"Good. Any problems?"

"No, of course not. Everything's fine." Erin sat on the couch and tossed her purse onto the table next to her coffee.

"What's your evaluation so far?"

"Well, he's a bit distracted, but I think he's pleasant. I'm confident we'll be on schedule soon."

"I'm counting on you, Erin. You're my best, but I don't want you to underestimate this assignment."

"No problem, Patricia. I can handle him. He's nothing more than a big kid."

"Right. Okay then, keep me informed."

"I will. Thanks."

Erin hung up the phone then slid it into her shorts pocket.

Spence vaulted over the back of the couch, landing next to her. "So, I'm a 'big kid,' eh?"

"Yes, you are."

"And that doesn't worry you?" he asked.

"No. Do you always eavesdrop on other people's phone calls?"

"Sometimes."

"Let's talk about your plans," she suggested.

"I never kiss and tell." Spence stretched out on the couch, putting his head in Erin's lap. She shoved him and he rolled onto the carpeted floor.

"I mean your plans for the book. How far along are you?"

Spence didn't answer. He crossed his arms behind his head and stared at Erin's legs.

"You are incredibly hard-headed, you know that?" She turned sideways and slipped her feet between the couch cushions, removing her legs from his line of sight. "I'm not here to goof around with you, as pleasant as that may be. I'm a professional editor and we've got a lot of work to do."

Her stomach growled. "After I eat," she added.

* * *

Foraging in the kitchen netted Erin a large bowl of cereal, which she followed with more coffee. She plugged in her laptop, sat at the end of the counter and looked through the dining room windows. It was another sunny day on the island and the shimmering water in the distance hypnotized her. Fingers poised over the keyboard, instead of logging into her Internet email account, she watched a father and son race along the beach. The little boy, about six years old, dragged a kite behind him. A border collie zipped around them, racing circle eights. She heard the little boy squeal in pleasure when the dog grabbed the kite in its teeth and ran behind the dunes.

The father swung his son into the air, then placed him on his shoulders. The squeals and giggles ebbed as they followed the dog behind the dunes.

"Cute kid, huh?" Spence stood behind the counter and stuffed part of a bagel into his mouth. "They're my neighbors."

"A sweet family," Erin said.

"Nah, it's a sad story. The wife died last year. Hit and run during the summer season. She was out jogging and some jerk killed her. Police never caught the man. Or woman. Who knows?"

"How horrible," Erin said, watching for the father and son on the empty beach. "I can imagine that in D.C. Everybody drives like a jerk there. But here? This is such a small place and it seems so quaint."

"Not in the summer. The place gets crazy with tourists and those of us who aren't in the service industry usually clear out."

"You don't live here year 'round? Where do you go?"

"I've got a cabin in Nevada, near Tahoe. Or I head offshore. Do a little cruising, maybe go to the islands."

Erin thought of the magazine in Patricia's office featuring Spence and a beautiful woman in a tropical setting.

"Must be a hard life," she sympathized, her pinched

lips contradicting her words. "Well, enough small talk. Let's get to work."

She slid a flash drive across the counter. "I'll need your notes and samples of your artwork. Why don't you save your files on this and we'll get started."

Spence picked up the gadget. "Yeah, well, that's going to be a problem."

Erin looked from her email login page. "Why?"

"I don't have any notes." Spence flipped the small plastic device towards Erin, and she caught it reflexively. She gripped her bottom lip between her teeth and narrowed her eyes.

"Don't smolder at me. I'm an artist. I don't do files and notes. I paint."

"How do you expect to write a book without notes?" she asked, pronouncing each word with menace.

"Isn't that why you're here? I make the pictures. You make the notes."

Erin stared out the window, no longer entranced by the beautiful day. She closed her eyes and sighed. "Okay, we know where we stand now. Square One."

She opened her eyes and turned towards Spence. "It's okay," she repeated, more for her own benefit than his. "Just give me samples of your artwork, everything you have, and I'll start an outline." She held out the flash drive again.

Spence took it and dropped it in his shirt pocket. "There's a guy in town who takes all my photos. I'll have him drop off my slides," he said.

Erin sipped her coffee. "I'd prefer them in digital format. On the flash drive. That's why I gave it to you."

He looked at his watch. "I'll see what he's got," he said. "Give me a couple days."

"Why?"

The question confused Spence. "Why what?"

"Why do I have to give him a couple days? What's wrong with today? It's Monday, right?"

Spence looked into space as if conjuring a calendar. "Yeah, but I won't be back until Wednesday."

Erin's jaw dropped. "What? Where are you going?"

"Fishing."

The one-word answer made Erin's blood boil.

"Fishing? Fishing! I didn't come all the way from Washington, D.C. to sit here and wait for you to get back from fishing. You are not going fishing!"

Spence backed away from her, hands raised at her tirade.

"Uh, yes I am. It's my boat and it's too late to change our plans."

Erin closed her eyes against the throb building in her temple. She regulated her breathing, grasping for a sense of calm. Yet another roadblock.

"What am I supposed to do while you're gone?" she asked, her voice low and angry. "Twiddle my thumbs?"

"Make yourself at home," Spence called as he headed down the hallway. He returned a minute later with a small duffle bag in one hand, his car keys in the other. He handed her a piece of paper. "Here's my cell phone number and the code for the front door. When I get back, I'll work like a dog for you. I mean, a puppy," he said, winking.

Erin snarled at the remark, recalling her conversation with Spence about not wanting a relationship. She pulled out her cell phone and punched the speed dial as he walked out the front door.

"Patricia? It's Erin. Something's come up."

To Erin's relief, Patricia accepted the delay, but gave the young woman another warning. "Well, if he's had this planned for a while, you can't do anything about it. I told you, this guy is hard to pin down."

Chagrinned, Erin promised to spend the next two days researching his background for the book's introduction.

With a hollow feeling of dread in her stomach, she approached Spence's quiet studio. Several canvases leaned against one wall, and the closet doors stood open. She arranged the paintings side-by-side along the walls, encircling the room. She sat on the floor and studied them, wondering what made his landscapes so popular. She knew little about art, but appreciated the simple beauty of the watercolors and the intricate elegance of the oils. Soft hues of blues and browns and greens dominated his work, and each one revealed a secret side of the rugged islands of the Outer Banks. Some of the paintings were landscapes, some featured people at work on the island. As she appraised the art, she felt a quiet sense of peacefulness. His art didn't excite. It relaxed. It seeped into the soul and spoke of the motionless corners of the marsh, the gentle sweep of the dune, the strength in the swaying sea oat.

She returned the paintings to their stack against the wall and went to the closet to snoop. Instead of regular-sized drawers, the closet contained cabinets with shallow trays. Each tray contained something different. One held fresh watercolor paper, another held the photographs he used when painting. She poked though the drawers, looking at assorted paint supplies and frame-making materials. One large cabinet contained photography equipment, mostly older SLR cameras, lenses and filters. Another cabinet held beach finds. She found broken sea shells, chipped sand dollars, and dried reeds and grasses. The man didn't collect perfection, she noted, recalling his words on the beach the previous night. In fact, it seemed he preferred the imperfect.

Satisfied she'd met the artist, Erin padded down the hall to Spence's bedroom, seeking the man behind the lazy smile. Once again, dread filled her stomach with butterflies. She didn't like sneaking and prying. She rationalized her behavior, though, as part of the "research" she'd promised Patricia she'd conduct.

She opened his bedroom door and stepped into the sun-filled room. It mirrored her own suite, except his messy king-sized bed didn't feature a satin comforter. It contained only rumpled sheets. Erin sat on the bed and spread a hand on the soft pillow-top mattress. She closed her eyes and took a deep breath, inhaling a tangy, soft scent. It reminded her of the ocean and sand. She shook her head to clear her mind, and stood. The lure of Spence's bedroom overwhelmed her and she decided she'd researched enough.

* * *

Erin paid the cashier and turned to the young man packing groceries into plastic bags. "Do you need help out to your car, ma'am?"

"No thanks," she said. "But let me ask you something. Is there a professional photographer on the island?"

The teen looked at the cashier. "I don't know. Hey, Frieda, is there a photographer around here?"

The older woman closed the cash register and yanked the receipt from the slot. She handed it, along with some loose change, to Erin. "Well, there's Scott Schultz. I don't how much of a 'professional' he is, but he develops film and does weddings."

Erin asked for directions, deciding to return to town that afternoon and visit the man's shop. Her immediate plans were to supply Spence's house with food and the sorbet wouldn't last a side trip.

Finding his mailbox and driveway were easier the second time around, and after making several trips ferrying groceries into the house, she sat on the stool and checked her cell phone for messages.

There were a couple of phone calls from Aidan, which she ignored. She glanced through her email on the small browser window, relieved nothing important loomed. Too often, former clients contacted her in need of reassurance before a book signing or an interview. It was aggravating, yet it stroked her ego, also. People valued her opinion.

She made a sandwich and a bowl of soup, then turned

on her laptop to read the latest news while she ate. Now that she'd met him, she couldn't resist typing Spence's name into an Internet search engine. Her eyes widened in disbelief when the first entry, an article from two hours earlier on Huffington Post, included a photograph of Spence on his fishing boat with two professional baseball players. One held a large fish as a trophy. The caption read, "Former Boston Red Sox player Nomar Garcioparra lands a marlin on a sport fishing trip in the Outer Banks with former Yankee and teammate Mike Wolfson and artist Stephen Spence. Not shown is ESPN announcer Karl Ravech, who shared this photo on his fan page."

He'd left several hours ago, yet, via the power of the Internet, Erin found him drifting in a boat in the Atlantic Ocean, within cell phone range. When he said a "fishing trip," she'd imagined him and a local friend in a squalid boat amid bloody bait and tangled lines, not an expensive outing with professional athletes.

For a moment, she felt envious. The photo, taken with a mobile phone and uploaded to a social media app, depicted a perfect spring day. The blue sky contrasted with the gleaming white hull of the expensive boat. The men wore board shorts and no shirts, their muscled torsos tanned in the sunlight. They wore designer sunglasses, had bright smiles and held large fishing poles. Spence sat grinning in a captain's seat, swiveled to face the other men. He held a beer in one hand, and a fish net in the other.

Well, at least he hadn't lied. He hadn't elaborated either. Erin wondered what it would be like to fish with famous people. Despite his laid-back appearance, Spence mingled with anyone. Erin felt smug that no beautiful models were on the fishing trip.

At the sound of giggling, she glanced out the sliding glass doors to the beach beyond. The little boy next door rolled down a sand dune, his dog nipping and tugging on his pants to stop him. As Erin watched, the boy ran up the hill, again and again, followed by the dog as they played their game.

Erin walked out the door and stood on the deck, shading her eyes in the sunlight as she looked for the boy's father. Surely, he wouldn't be playing alone. She saw a hunched figure of a man sitting near the shore, watching the waves. He sat motionless, staring at the horizon, his shoulders bent in sadness. That is, until the boy raced in the sand toward him and launched onto his father's back. The two rolled into the waves laughing and the collie joined them, leaping and barking its excitement.

She glanced at her watch and realized she'd been watching the family for half an hour. If she didn't hurry, the photographer's shop would close. She turned off the laptop, picked up her handbag and left the house for the small town of Ocracoke.

"Becky," the GPS avatar, once again guided her with expert efficiency through the unmarked roads crisscrossing the island. Erin parked in front of the business, an old white cottage converted into a shop. Before entering, she paused at the large display window to look at the camera equipment and portraits on exhibit. Then she walked into the shop and a small bell announced her arrival.

An older man shuffled from the backroom, carrying a hammer. He looked like a carpenter, dressed in a plaid cotton shirt and a pair of scruffy jeans. He grinned in welcome. "Good afternoon," he said, placing the hammer on a stool. "Can I help you?"

She approached the counter, a cautious smile pasted on her face. "My name is Erin Andersen. I'm an editor working with Mr. Spence on his book."

The man frowned. He looked confused.

Erin forged ahead. "He might not have mentioned it to anyone yet, but he's under contract with McDowell Publishing for a book about his artwork. I'm not sure if you can help me, but before he left this morning, he said his 'photographer friend' had the slides of his artwork we need for production. I'm hoping you are this friend," she said, with a winsome look.

Scott Schultz's frown disappeared. "Oh, I think I understand. Maybe not. What can I do for you?"

"Do you have negatives of Mr. Spence's paintings?"

He nodded, still not convinced he should speak with her.

"That's great," she said, her smile brightening. "I need to send copies to my art director as soon as possible. Can you help me with that?"

The man hemmed. "Well, I don't know. Not without his permission, of course."

Erin flashed a grin. "Not a problem. Give me a moment," she said, pulling out her mobile phone. If Spence's boat was close enough to shore that his friends could upload photos to the Internet, then he should be close enough to talk.

The phone rang several times and Erin's spirits sank. Then, she heard his voice, laughing. "You got me," he said as way of greeting.

"Mr. Spence, this is Erin Andersen," she said.

He yelled, "Hey, you guys be quiet. I can't hear."

Erin waited for him to return. "Who's this?" he asked.

"Erin Andersen," she repeated, glancing at the shop owner. "I'm with Scott Schultz and he needs your permission to make duplicate slides for the art department."

The phone was quiet for a moment, then Spence chuckled. "You're a little dynamo. Can't wait for me to get back, can you?" The tone of his voice intimated she couldn't wait for him for various reasons, none of them editing a book.

She cleared her throat. "I'm going to hand the phone to Mr. Shultz. Please tell him to accommodate my needs." As she passed the phone, she heard Spence offer, "I'll accommodate your needs, sweetheart."

Erin turned her back so the man could speak in private. She moved to a far wall and studied the various photographs hanging there. A minute later, Scott handed her the mobile phone. "He wants to talk to you."

"Yes?" she asked, slipping the phone between her ear and shoulder.

"So, how are you doing? Miss me already?" The question was coy.

"The sun has addled your brains if you think I miss you," she said. "I'll let you get back to your friends and your little party. Tell Mike Wolfson I said 'hello,'" she added.

This caught Spence by surprise. "You know Mike? Hey Mike," he yelled over his shoulder. "You know a cute little gal named Erin Andersen?"

She gritted her teeth. "I am not a 'cute little gal,'" she said. She heard a muted conversation between the men. "Hell yeah, is that her? Let me talk to her," Mike said, his voice slurring.

Spence put the phone back to his chin and said, "Nah, he said he don't know you. Gotta go, sweetheart. I'll see you tomorrow night." Then the phone went silent.

From his perch on the stool behind the counter, Scott Schultz watched Erin grimace and slide the phone into her pants pocket. When she looked up and caught his eye, she blushed.

He nodded. "Yep, I guess you know him."

CHAPTER FIVE

Erin spent a restless night alone in Spence's house. She read in bed until after midnight, then tossed and turned for several more hours. She didn't like to lose control, but every conversation she had with him left her reeling. She wanted to deny the attraction, but Spence conjured feelings she'd prefer to ignore. On one hand, he flattered her with his cajoling and flirtatious manner. On the other, he infuriated her with his indolence and lack of concern.

Most of her clients were scholars, compulsive obsessive types she understood since she experienced a mild version of the disorder. She needed control, and it distressed her that Spence couldn't care less.

She crawled out of bed the next morning, bleary eyed and resentful. She played her cell phone messages while she ate a bowl of cereal. Aidan left another communication, this one belligerent and demanding she return his call. With grim satisfaction, she punched in his phone number. When he answered, she snarled at him. "What gives you the right to call me and tell me what to do? Don't you ever do that again, you hear me?"

Confused, Aidan apologized. "I'm sorry, Erin. I was

worried about you. I haven't heard from you in several days. I didn't know if you were all right or not."

She closed her eyes in resignation. "I know. It's okay. I've had a rough couple days and I'm tired. My client is not the easiest person to work with," she said, rubbing her forehead.

"Why don't you pass on this job and come home?" he asked.

"No, I'm not going to do that," she said, taking a deep breath as she defended her decision. "Patricia depends upon me to get the job done, even if it means working with the obstinate ones," she said, referring to difficult clients.

"Well, I'm here if you need to talk," Aidan offered.

His soothing voice calmed her and they spoke about his work in the lab. She let him lead the conversation, not wanting to talk about Stephen Spence and his unsettling behavior. She rang off with a promise to call him in a couple days. Despite the hurt and disappointment he'd caused during the final year of their marriage, she still cared for Aidan.

She decided a stroll would help clear the cobwebs, so she slipped on a pair of flip-flops and walked out the door to the deck. She left the screen door unlocked this time and after several minutes of searching, found the trail through the sea grass that led to the beach.

When she reached the shore, she walked in the waves, her flip flops dangling in her hand. She walked about a half a mile, before turning back. When she neared the house, she paused in the shallows, letting the waves bury her feet in the sand. She felt the tiny coquina shells tickling her toes. She startled, jumping out of the sand when a soft voice spoke next to her.

"I like do that too," the small boy said. He kicked off his sandals and rolled his pants legs over his knees. Then he walked into the shallows and wiggled his toes until the sand covered them. He chortled, which brought his black-

and-white border collie careening over the sand dune. The frisky dog joined the fun, bouncing in the water and splashing Erin and the boy. They laughed together at its antics.

The boy measured her, approval in his brilliant blue eyes. "I like the way you laugh," he said. "My name is Jonathan. What's yours?"

"My name is Erin," she said, smiling at the imp. "I'm visiting Mr. Spence."

"I know him. He lives in the big gray house," Jonathan said. "He's a nice man. My daddy likes him a lot."

"Yes, he is a nice man," she agreed, looking around. "Where's your daddy? Isn't he here with you today?"

At that moment, she heard Jonathan's father calling for him. The little boy looked sheepish. "Over here, Daddy," he called.

He turned to Erin, a frown darkening his face. "I forgot to tell him me and Moxie were playing outside. Boy, I'm going to be in trouble now."

Erin watched as his father crested the dune, lifting a hand in welcome. She hoped he didn't assume the worst, and be worried that she was a monster trying to steal his child. The little boy understood and slipped his small hand into hers. "Don't worry. He's not mean. I'm not really in trouble," he said.

As his father approached, he called out, "Hi Daddy. This is Erin. She lives next door with Mr. Spence." He whistled the last word through a missing front tooth.

Erin blushed at the words from the mouth of babes. "I'm not living there," she said as the man stepped closer. "I'm visiting." Her voice trailed off when he stopped, towering over her. She looked into sad eyes, and melted. The man bent and picked up his son. Erin let go of his little hand and watched as the man hugged the child tight to his chest, his eyes closing in relief.

"Don't ever do that again," he whispered into his son's ear.

"I won't, Daddy," the little boy whispered back.

Erin couldn't help herself. She clasped her hands to her chest, her lips parting as she gasped at the poignancy. She shivered when he glanced over his son's head and caught her staring. He backed away, then swung the boy onto his hip. He snapped his fingers and Moxie sat at his feet, a ball of quivering, silky fur.

Jonathan rested his head on his father's shoulder and turned towards Erin. "Isn't she pretty, Daddy? Like Mommy."

Erin blinked. She swallowed. She couldn't speak. Spence told her about the family's tragedy and to be face-to-face with people who'd experienced such horror overwhelmed her. With the exception of her divorce, her life was a happy one filled with work and satisfaction. She'd never lost a loved one, except for Aidan. But even he wouldn't go away.

The man dipped his head, his blonde hair falling in his face and shielding his eyes. Erin watched him bite his lip, noting the indentation there. He bit his lip a lot.

She stepped aside and turned towards the water. "Well, I've got to be going now. It was nice to meet you, Jonathan. And you too, Moxie," she said, bending to pat the dog's head. It lifted its muzzle and grinned at her. "Goodbye."

As moved towards the house, the man spoke. "I'm Paul Shepherd," he said, extending a hesitant hand to shake hers. Erin paused and placed her hand in his. He pulled his hand back as if burned, then looked away.

She touched her chest. "Erin Andersen. I'm working with Mr. Spence on a project, so I'll probably see you around." She glanced at her watch. "Well, I've got to be going now. It was nice meeting you both."

As she retreated, she heard the boy whisper to his father, then he yelled, "Bye! See you tomorrow." She lifted a hand to wave, then slogged through the sand and sea oats back to the house.

Once inside, she peeked through the window and watched the small family walk the shoreline, hand-in-hand. The dog ran ahead and made them laugh as it pranced in the waves. Soon, they were out of sight. Erin exhaled, not realizing she'd been holding her breath. She didn't know how to act around people who'd lost a loved one. She felt awkward and uncomfortable, worrying she would do or say the wrong thing.

She heard the front door open and a high-pitched voice call out, "Yoo hoo. Anybody home?"

Erin leaned towards the hall and watched as an older woman came into the house, closing the door behind her. She tossed her large straw beach bag on the floor next to the door. "Spence? Are you up?"

The woman saw Erin and froze. "Well, hello there," she said, a smile creasing her tanned, lined face. "Don't mind me. I'm Abby, the housekeeper. I'll be in and out in no time."

Erin blushed. "No, that's okay. Take your time," she told the woman. "Mr. Spence isn't here right now."

When Abby winked at her, she realized she'd only confirmed the woman's suspicions.

"No, what I mean is, I'm working with Mr. Spence. I'm here temporarily."

Abby bustled into the hallway and pressed on a panel, revealing a hidden closet. She withdrew a broom and a bucket with cleaning supplies tucked in it. Erin moved to the far side of the island when Abby came into the kitchen. The woman settled into her silent routine, lifting the dirty cereal bowl out of the sink and opening the dishwasher.

Erin rushed to her side. "Oh, I'm sorry. That's my bowl. I'll wash it and put it away," she apologized.

Abby stood, placing her hand on her back. She pinned dark brown eyes on Erin. "Are you planning on cleaning everything before I get a chance to?"

Erin shook her head, frozen in the woman's glare like a deer in headlights.

"Good. Because it's my job, not yours. You go about whatever business you got here and I'll go about mine," the woman compromised. She looked around with suspicion. "Where is the rascal?"

"Fishing."

Abby blew a puff of air then rolled her eyes. "Typical. And he just left you here alone? When's he coming back?

"Tonight."

"Mmmm hmmm." Abby studied Erin, flicking her knowing eyes up and down, noting her casual clothes and sandy feet. "Well, listen here ..., what did you say your name was?"

"Erin."

"Mmmm hmmm, well, listen here Erin. I come by twice a week and it takes me a couple hours to get things straight here. Spence isn't a pig, so I'm in and out. I don't talk to him. He don't talk to me. We stay out of each other's way and that's the way we like it. No offense, but I can't work with someone standing over my shoulder. You got something else to do? Somewhere else to go?"

"No."

Abby shook her head in resignation.

"Actually, I do have somewhere to go," Erin said, backing up and pointing a thumb. "I'll be back later. You'll probably be gone by then."

She raced into her room for her handbag and fished out the car keys. Geesh, between a missing client, an irate ex-husband, a playful little boy, and a bossy cleaning woman, Erin didn't know which direction to go.

She decided to enlist Becky's help once she reached the car. She plugged in the GPS receiver and punched buttons, searching for local shops and restaurants. A few minutes later, she drove on Route 12 heading into the small village of Ocracoke. She parked near the harbor, and decided to pass on renting a bike. Instead, she walked and enjoyed the sights. After a long visit to the bookstore, she stopped by the local coffee shop for a beverage and a bagel.

Refreshed, she visited the local art galleries and antique stores. After hours of walking, she stopped by the ice cream store, but the harried staff ignored her and she waited ten minutes for someone to take her order. She finally got service and asked for a cone of strawberry ice cream. Then she ambled to the harbor and visited the fish house, watching as local watermen unloaded their catches into large, ice-filled coolers. The ice cream melted in the warm spring afternoon, dripping down her hand and onto the pier. A pelican waddled around her, turning its head to stare quizzically at the dripping mass of pink napkins in her fist.

"No, it's not a fish," Erin said, shaking her hand over a trashcan and depositing the slimy mess. "But it's just as nasty," she added.

Above her head, sea gulls screeched and floated, having followed the fishing boats into the harbor. She squinted into the bright light, then realized she hadn't used sunscreen again. Her arms and legs were pink and the back of her neck was getting red. She ducked into a gift shop and walked up and down the air conditioned aisles looking for sunscreen and a baseball cap. After shelling out more than twenty dollars for the over-priced island merchandise, she continued to explore the village.

She chatted with shop owners, including several who carried signed, limited edition prints by "Ocracoke's own Stephen Spence."

"He is such a sweetheart," one older woman said, adding with a wicked grin, "If I were thirty years younger, I'd give him a run for his money."

The assistant manager, an old man, nudged the owner. "You mean forty years."

She laughed, the clear sound ringing through the gallery. "Who's counting and who cares? That man is something else."

Erin's tugged the corners of her grimace into a crooked smile and continued browsing the shop. She had to admit,

Spence's prints were spectacular and the most impressive art inventory the local shops carried. His skill surpassed other local painters, whose work hung in the back of most shops.

The afternoon slipped away and soon shops were closing for the evening. Erin made a loop around the harbor before heading back to her car. She inhaled the aroma of two-cycle engine oil, diesel, salt spray and fish. Then, she heard a familiar laugh in the distance and stumbled over a sloppy dock line, coiled around a cleat. When she regained her footing, she looked around until she heard the sound again. Three piers over, a shirtless Stephen Spence unloaded fishing poles from a large, white fishing boat. It had a tall structure crowned with radar dishes and antennas, making the boat look top heavy.

Erin made her way towards Spence, pausing at the entrance of the pier where a sign warned trespassers to stay clear of the private boats. As she hesitated, Spence jumped from the boat and handed a cooler to a tall, dark-haired man with a hawk nose. She couldn't hear their conversation but they laughed once more and the tall man walked away, heading Erin's way. Behind him, Spence caught a glimpse of her and waved.

"Well, hey there sweetheart. Come on down and look at my boat," he invited.

Erin passed the tall man with a brief nod, then continued on to Spence.

As she approached him, he called out, "Nomar! Hey man, make sure you rub those fillets with olive oil before you blacken them."

Erin paused. Nomar? As in Nomar Garcioparra?

As she approached Spence, she noticed his sun-streaked tousled hair. His feet were bare and he wore a faded, torn pair of board shorts. He looked liked a beach bum, with the emphasis on "bum."

He looked gorgeous.

Spence jumped back on the boat and held a hand for

her, waiting for her to close the short distance. "Come aboard," he said, cupping his hand in invitation. "I'm still putting things away. You can help."

Erin put her hand in his and stepped onto the gunwale of the boat. It rocked and she felt her balance shift. Afraid she would fall between the boat and the pier, she squeaked. Spence caught her around the waist and plucked her from her perch. "Don't worry, sweetheart. I gotcha."

On solid footing, Erin backed out of his arms. "I'm not your sweetheart," she said, tossing her handbag onto a nearby cushion.

Spence laughed until a coughing fit started, then he punched his chest a couple times. "Man," he said, tears coming to his eyes. "I'm not used to those Cuban cigars."

Erin frowned. "I didn't know you smoked."

But Spence was heading to the bow of the boat and didn't hear her. She watched as he hoisted a yellow and white bait bucket, water rushing from its holes. He slid a hand inside and pulled out several shrimp. Looking up, he caught sight of a fat old pelican waiting on the pier. Spence tossed the shrimp and the pelican caught them with ease. As soon as he reached back into the bucket, sea gulls spotted him and began to circle. He tossed the unused bait, one shrimp at a time, into the air and the gulls caught each one. He threw one last handful to the pelican, then dumped the water from the bucket.

He untied the bucket's line from the stanchion and returned aft, where Erin waited. As he walked past her, she noticed a fine white powder dusting the freckles scattered on his shoulders and back. "What is that stuff?" she asked.

At his confused look, she wiped a finger on him and held it up.

"Ah, salt," he said. "Haven't had a shower in a couple days."

Erin looked at her finger and then rubbed it on the leg of her shorts, her lip curling. She put her hands on her hips and turned in a semi-circle, watching as he moved around the boat, closing lockers, retying fenders, testing dock lines. She spied the ladder leading to the super structure. "May I go up there?" she asked, pointing.

At his nod, she started up the ladder. When she neared the top, she turned and caught him watching. "Are you looking at my bum again?"

"Yes ma'am," he said. "You've got nice legs."

She shook her head, not as disgusted as she'd like to pretend. "Well don't." She climbed the ladder and pulled herself into the small caged area where a white captain's chair faced an enormous panel filled with electronic gauges. She sat in the chair and swiveled, enjoying the view of the harbor and marina from above. She had to admit, it was pretty cool. From her new vantage point, Erin studied Spence as he cleaned the boat. She admired the corded muscles of his arms and back as he hefted a plastic garbage bag onto the pier. It clunked with the distinct sound of empty cans and bottles.

"Hope you're hungry," he called out.

"Why? Are you taking me out to dinner again?"

"Nah, got some fresh fish," he said. "We caught some tuna."

"And you're telling me this because ...?" Erin let the question taper off, emphasizing her lack of interest in fresh fish.

Spence mounted the steps to the structure, then leaned first one way, then the next, making the boat list. Erin clutched the captain's chair, unsettled by the slight rocking motion. "Quit that!" she demanded. "It's not funny."

He jumped off the ladder and laughed again. "You're a prissy thing, aren't ya? Don't like fish. Don't like rocking boats. What else you don't like?"

"Lazy people!" she said, then swung onto the ladder and clambered down. "Bullies. Pigs. Jerks," she continued before reaching the bottom and turning to face Spence. "Want me to go on?"

He held his hands up, palms out. "Truce," he begged.

"I'm sorry for scaring you."

Erin crossed her arms and frowned at him. "You didn't scare me."

"Maybe. Just a little?" he suggested.

She glanced around as if interested in anything except him. "Where's Mike Wolfson? I thought you went out with him? And that other guy?"

"Karl," he supplied. "I let them off at Kitty Hawk. Saves 'em a ferry ride. So, how you know Mike?"

Erin picked up her handbag. "He's from my hometown. He went to school with my sister. Now, show me the best way to get off the boat, please."

Spence scooped her in his arms, stepped onto the gunwale and then down to the pier in one fluid motion.

Erin gasped and clutched at his arms, her hands slipping on the salty residue. "How dare you!"

"You asked for the best way. I showed ya," he said. He tossed a cooler onto his shoulder. "Hand me that trash bag," he added.

Erin lifted the bag by the yellow plastic ties, hefted it, then gave it to him. "I'm amazed you caught any fish. Is this thing filled with beer bottles and cans?"

"Aw nah," he assured her. "We don't drink that much. There's some water bottles in there and soda. I'd never drive 'Belinda' drunk."

She followed in his wake, looking back at the boat's transom and the rich illustration there of a pinup girl and the name "Belinda."

She couldn't resist. "Who's Belinda?"

"My first grade teacher," he said. "You never forget your first love."

CHAPTER SIX

Erin wished she had more to report. "I'm sorry, Patricia. It's been a hectic few days getting settled in," she said. She hated to make excuses, too. "Mr. Spence is back now and we're waiting for slides of his art. They'll be here this week. I've been interviewing him for the introduction, and I spoke with several gallery owners in town about his work." She didn't mention she spent the afternoon ambling from one shop to the next.

Once again, she worked at the kitchen island, reviewing her email on her laptop. A curt note from Patricia had her dialing the office first thing in the morning.

"Yes, everything is fine," she said, nodding to Spence as he shook the half-and-half carton at her. He poured some into a coffee cup, stopping when she raised her index finger. Then he lifted the sugar bowl and repeated the process. He poured the steaming brew into the cup and stirred, the spoon tinkling against the ceramic sides.

"Yes, I can hear you," Erin said. Spence stirred softer, then placed the spoon in the sink and pushed the overfull cup towards his editor.

She picked up the cup and sipped. "Ummmm. Yes, yes, I know. Right away. What?" Erin raised her eyes to

Spence, then placed the cup on the counter. She swiveled on the stool and looked out the sliding glass door. "Yes, he's much better. He's settling down and we're making progress. Yes. I will, thank you. Goodbye Patricia."

She hung up the phone, then lifted the cup of coffee to her lips. She closed her eyes and let the fragrant steam bathe her face.

On the other side of the counter, Spence lifted his cup and drank. "So, I'm 'much better,' eh?"

She scrunched her nose at him. "I had to tell her something. What did you think I'd say? 'Oh, we ate blackened fish and rice and drank too much beer and fell asleep in front of the television.' That would go over real well," she said, her voice tinged with sarcasm.

"So you admit it was good."

She rolled her eyes. "It was okay."

"C'mon, admit it. You liked it."

"I said it was okay. It doesn't taste like seafood when you coat it with all those spices and burn it."

"Blacken, not burn," he corrected. "Burned is what you are. Don't you have any sunscreen?"

She looked at her red forearms, then back at her laptop screen. "Yes." Then she ignored him and checked through the rest of her emails, sipping coffee in between responses. The sound of knocking on the sliding glass door startled her.

Spence walked towards the door and slid it open. "Hey buddy," he said, letting Jonathan and Moxie into the house. He glanced towards the beach and waved at Paul. He left the door open, letting the father know his son would return shortly.

Jonathan, however, ignored Spence and skipped to Erin. She swiveled on the bar stool and smiled at the little boy.

"Hi," she said, her voice light and sweet. "What are doing here? Where's your father?"

She sat higher on the seat, looking through the sliding

glass door for the familiar blonde man.

"Me and Moxie and Daddy are going to build sandcastles today and we'd like you to judge them," he said. "So, I'm supposed to tell you that you can come out and play in about an hour. That's how long it will take us."

He looked over his shoulder at Spence. "You can play, too."

Erin's smile froze and she turned to Spence.

"Will do, buddy," he said, looking at his watch. "We'll see you at about, say, ten o'clock. Okay?"

Jonathan nodded, his head bouncing up and down, and Moxie barked. Then he flashed another gap-toothed grin at Erin. "See you soon," he said, whistling.

Then the two dashed out the back door, slid under the rail and into the sea grass. They were invisible except for the waving brown fronds, then came back into sight at the crest of the sand dune.

Erin heard the little boy call in the distance, "She said, 'Yes!'"

Spence closed the door. "Looks like you got an admirer."

Erin still had a frozen smile pasted on her face.

"You can relax now," Spence said.

"I don't know much about kids," she said, with a trace of panic in her voice. "Except for my sister's kids."

"They're people, only shorter. Just be nice and make sure he wins the sandcastle contest," he said.

"We have too much work to do," she said, shuffling through sheaves of notepaper on the counter. "I can't be gallivanting on the beach all day."

Spence opened the refrigerator. "It's only an hour," he said. "Hey, you got eggs. I'll make us some omelets."

* * *

An hour later, Erin knelt between two castles, looking from one to the other with a serious expression.

"And see, mine's got turrets and a moat," Jonathan said. "Dad's got a moat too, but it's not as deep as mine."

Erin studied the structures, squinting one eye and scrunching her lips at the details. Then she nodded as if making her decision. She tried to stand, but Moxie picked that moment to leap over Paul's castle and at the back of Erin's knees, knocking her onto her backside. Paul's castle crumbled and the dog sprang aside, but not before swiping a pink, wet tongue across Erin's cheek.

"Moxie! No!" Jonathan screeched. "Bad dog."

But Moxie didn't listen. The dog crouched and wiggled its haunches, then jumped back into Erin's lap and bathed her cheeks. Erin lifted her face out of reach and pushed the dog aside.

Spence fell to his knees, laughing so hard he held his stomach.

Paul bit his lip, his hands shoved into the pockets of his cargo shorts.

Erin sat up, then dusted her legs, wincing at the sting of sand brushing her sunburn. "It's okay, Jonathan," she said. "I had already made my decision. I picked your castle."

Jonathan threw his short arms around her neck and hugged, choking her in the process. "That's good because I worked real hard. I wanted you to like mine," he said.

Erin caught the little boy in her arms and squeezed. "You are such a cutie," she said.

Paul ruffled his son's white blonde hair. "Okay, Jonathan. Tell Miss Erin goodbye. It's time for your nap," he said, his eyes shining.

"Aww, do I have to?"

"Yes, those are the rules," Paul replied, his voice soft and kind. He whistled for Moxie and the dog bounded to his feet and crouched.

Erin looked from the obedient dog to the father, a wry grin on her face. "That dog does exactly what you want, doesn't it?"

Paul smiled. "Most of the time," he said.

Spence offered Erin a hand and pulled her to her feet. She tossed a sandal in the process and Moxie caught it in mid-flight, then carried it to his owner.

Paul held out the shoe. "Sometimes, I don't even have to ask him."

Spence stepped between them and took the shoe. Erin scowled.

"We'll see you later, buddy," Spence said, patting Jonathan on the shoulder. "You too, Paul." He moved beside Erin, his presence overwhelming and annoying her.

As soon as Paul and Jonathan were out of earshot, she turned on him. "You're not subtle," she said. "What's the big idea, acting all macho like that? I'm not your property."

"Who me?" Spence wore an incredulous expression. "I don't know what you're talking about. Anyway, let's go. We've got work to do."

Erin glowered at his back all the way to the house.

CHAPTER SEVEN

Spence alternated his time between painting in his studio and working on the book with Erin at the kitchen counter. Erin picked up the new slides and a DVD filled with scanned images from Scott Schultz, then imported the data into her laptop.

She felt good about the progress they'd made so far, collaborating several hours a day. When Spence worked in the studio, she caught up on correspondence with former clients, discussed layout possibilities with the publishing house's production department, and relaxed on the beach, reading. This continued for one week, then Spence showed signs of restlessness.

Erin sat at the kitchen counter, her workspace cluttered with printouts, slides and empty coffee cups. "Let's talk about your categories next," she said, focusing on the laptop screen as she divvied the images into separate folders.

Spence scowled. "What categories? What are you talking about?

"You're kidding, right?"

Spence pushed off his stool and refilled his coffee cup. "No. What kind of categories? Categories of what?"

"Your art," she said, impatience creeping into her voice. "You know what I mean. You've got landscapes with no animals, then animals prominent in a natural setting. Next you've got paintings of buildings and places, and then you have people working. You know, the fishermen unloading their boats. The carpenter. The heron in the marsh. All of your paintings seem to fall into these types. I figured you meant to do it. I mean, it's pretty obvious," she said.

"Well, no," he said. "Not really."

She tilted her head, a quizzical look on her face, then turned the laptop so he could see the screen. "I've made four new folders and I've placed all of your paintings into the categories I see. Take a look and let me know what you think."

She sat back on the stool and watched as his face changed from guarded to confused, then to reluctant acceptance. He shrugged, then turned the computer back to Erin. "Looks okay to me."

She blinked. "So, you agree now that your art falls into several categories, right?"

At his slight nod, she continued. "Now that we've segregated them, we need to write new chapters for each new category. We'll incorporate these into the existing outline and ...," she stopped speaking when Spence walked to the sliding glass door and opened it. "I'm sorry, am I keeping you from something?" She found it difficult not to sneer.

Spence didn't answer. Instead, he walked outside and sat in the hammock.

Erin thought about confronting him, but something held her back. He seemed unsettled and she wondered if it had to do with her observations about the paintings. Could he really be that oblivious?

Erin closed the laptop then followed him outside. She went behind the bar and withdrew two icy beers from the small refrigerator. Without asking, she uncapped the bottles and held one out to him. Then she went back to the bar and hopped up, crossing her legs.

Spence rocked, one hand tossed behind his head, the other cradling the beer. He lifted the bottle to his lips, a thoughtful expression on his face. Ten minutes passed before he spoke.

"I didn't know," he said. "Here I thought I was spontaneous or something. I never believed that 'creative genius' crap some people said, but I thought I knew what I was doing."

He took a long pull on the beer, draining the contents. "Guess I'm not all that special, huh? Don't know what I'm doing after all," he said. He dropped the empty bottle to the deck.

Erin sipped her beer. Her knees were tingling from the sun. She didn't want to burn like her first day on the island, so she jumped off the bar and approached the sliding glass door.

"Spence, I'm going inside to take a nap. Don't stay out here all afternoon worrying about something that doesn't even matter. We all do things subconsciously, especially artists. You're intuitive, not premeditated. I get that. Obviously, these themes resonate with you and that's why you stick with them," she said. "I'll set my clock. We'll go out for dinner."

She was offering an olive branch, for what, she didn't know. Somehow, she'd wounded Spence. If something as simple as putting his art into a category distressed him, what would he do if she broke a plate? Ruined his shirt in the washing machine? Wrecked his car? He exasperated her and she felt so tired. Men and their fragile egos. Get over it, she wanted to scream.

Three hours later, Erin awoke refreshed and calm. She found Spence on the deck, still rocking in the hammock. Several more bottles had joined the empty one beside him. Twilight tinged the sky with pinks and purple and she heard the steady sound of waves in the distance.

"Do you need to take a shower before dinner?" she asked, trying to motivate him.

Spence turned to look at her, his face bemused. "I'm sailing south tomorrow."

Erin found it hard to catch her breath. "What? Are you nuts? You can't leave me here and sail off into the sunset."

"Well, you'll have to come with me," he said, rising from the hammock. She followed him into the dark, cool house.

"That's ridiculous. I'm not going anywhere," she said. "We've got to work on your book."

He opened the refrigerator and looked at the contents, his back to her. "We can do that on the boat. You sail?"

"Spence! Get serious," she begged. "We've been doing so well. We need to keep on schedule."

He closed the refrigerator door. "You'll get the hang of it," he said, ignoring her remarks. "Guess I better order some provisions."

Erin lost her appetite. She raised her fists. "Grrr! You drive me crazy," she said through clenched teeth. She grabbed her handbag and car keys. "Feed yourself. I'm out of here."

She stormed from the house, slamming the door. Spence heard the SUV's engine start and the wheels spin in the sand, kicking up shells in her haste to depart.

He pulled his cell phone from his shirt pocket. "Suzy Q? It's Spence," he said when the party answered. "I'm going to need some things for tomorrow morning."

* * *

"Pack light. Shorts, shirts, a bathing suit. Actually, leave your clothes here. Just bring your bikini."

Erin frowned. She'd returned to a quiet, dark house the night before. Instead of looking for Spence, she'd locked her bedroom door and read until two o'clock. She tossed and turned for another hour, then fell into a fitful sleep. He'd knocked on her door after seven, waking her. She stood in the bedroom doorway, dressed in a long T-shirt, her hair a frowsy mess.

"Spence, I'm not going anywhere. We have to work on the book."

"Plenty of time on the way. Come on, let's get your bag packed," he said, stepping into her room. He went to the closet and opened a drawer. She watched as he tossed clothing onto the bed.

"Hey! Get out of there. Stop that!" She smacked at his hand. "I am not going anywhere with you."

But then Erin thought back to her meeting with Patricia and how the book advance paid for the sailboat. No book meant no boat. Maybe that could be the hook to get him motivated. So what if she spent a couple days on a sailboat? In fact, being on a boat meant he couldn't get away and she'd have his complete attention.

"Okay, fine. I'll pack. Where did you put my suitcase?"

He disappeared and came back with a small canvas duffle bag. He tossed it to her and said, "Use this. Takes up less room on the boat."

Erin compared the bag and the mass of clothes on the bed. She raised an eyebrow at Spence.

"You don't need much."

He jumped on the bed and crossed his arms behind his head, watching her wade through the pile of silky underwear.

"Don't you have anything better to do?" she asked, hesitating.

"Better than looking at lady's underwear? Nope. I keep a bag on the boat so I'm always good to go."

She grabbed a handful and stuffed them in the bag. She added shorts and shirts, her toothbrush and toiletries.

"Fine. I'm ready."

"Got your bathing suit?"

"Yes."

"Good girl. Let's go."

He picked up her bag and walked away. She was not accustomed to being impetuous and tried to think of what else she might need. A bathing suit wasn't even on the list.

"Hold on. I need my laptop," she called out. She grabbed her briefcase and followed him. She paused in the living room, then dropped her laptop case on the table.

"Wait. We need to get something straight before we go."

Spence halted, his hand resting on the door knob. "What?"

Erin frowned, her lips pursing. "I suppose I can work on a boat, but I'll have to be able to do some research. And, I have to keep in touch with my office."

"Don't worry. I've got satellite Internet on the boat. We'll be sliding down the coast, so you'll have great reception. I'm sure whatever you need is available on the 'net."

"You have it all worked out, don't you?"

He winked, his face creasing in a good-natured smile. Erin felt a slow flush work up her neck.

* * *

Spence pulled into an empty parking place at the marina. "Better leave the keys with the car. Just in case." He lifted the floor mat and dropped the keys.

"Just in case? What do you mean?"

"In case we don't come back."

Erin stared at him, open mouthed.

"I don't mean we'll sink," he assured her. "I mean, maybe we'll keep going. I don't know, maybe we'll wind up in the Mediterranean. Ever been to Monaco?"

"You jest."

"We'll see."

She considered the situation. She was paid to make him work. He could work on a boat, on an island, in a casino for all she cared.

"Let's get this straight, Spence. This is not a holiday. I'm here on assignment, and you have a contract. So long as you agree to work whenever I say, I'll go with you. If not, then I have to go home and tell Mrs. McDowell there's no book."

"Agreed."

He led her down the weathered pier, toward the larger slips where his catamaran, "Fusion," was made fast. Erin squinted at the giant white multihull then at her duffle bag. She could have brought ten suitcases aboard the boat.

"Did this really cost $500,000?"

"Who told you that?" he asked, taking her canvas tote and tossing it into the cockpit.

"Umm, I forget."

"It's a bit more than that," he said, stretching one long, tanned leg to the stepped transom. He turned and held out a hand for her. "Closer to a million."

Erin gasped. "No way!"

Spence smiled and tugged her hand, forcing her to step off the pier and onto the boat. He guided her hand to a lifeline and took her laptop case. "Why don't you get settled in? I've got to do a few things," he said, looking over his shoulder. "Ah, there she is."

Erin followed his eyes and saw a young woman walking towards the boat, pulling a wagon. She had a baby perched on her hip, its blonde hair transparent in the bright sunlight.

"Hey Suzy-Q. Thanks for the grub," he said, shoving the laptop back into Erin's hands and reaching for the baby. The woman smiled and handed Spence the giggling child, its arms outstretched.

Spence swung the baby, clad only in a disposable diaper, in a circle before tossing it in the air. He caught the infant deftly, and then tucked it under his left arm like a football.

Suzy smiled, not at all worried with Spence's

mishandling of her baby. She eyed Erin with curiosity, then with amusement, as Spence once again swung the baby, this time upside down holding its ankles.

"Spence! That's not how you treat a baby!" Erin's voice was laced with horror. She tossed her laptop onto the cockpit table, then she pulled the giggling baby out of his outstretched hands. She rocked it in her arms. "There, there, don't cry."

The baby wasn't crying; however, and her dancing blue eyes enchanted Erin. She stroked her tiny, blonde curls, then glanced at Suzy, an apology on her lips.

"Don't worry; she loves it," Suzy said. Then, turning her attention to Spence, Suzy pulled a piece of paper out of her back pocket and handed it to him. "Here's the list of the supplies you wanted. I had Henry fill the water tanks and top off your fuel. Run the exhaust fan for a few minutes, though, before starting the engines. Also, the cooler was empty, so I restocked it.

"You've got plenty of soda and beer. Well, maybe not enough beer for you. Also, your mother said if you want your air tanks filled, you're going to have to do it yourself. She's having breakfast with a friend today and isn't opening the shop until this afternoon."

"Nah, that's all right. I'm not diving on this trip. Just a little snorkeling. Were you able to get everything?"

Suzy pulled the wagon to the edge of the pier and started pulling out plastic grocery bags, handing them across the divide to Spence.

"No, we don't have fresh cherries. You'll have to use canned. And you'll have to make do with rib eye instead of porterhouse. Speaking of steak, check your propane. If you need any, ring your bell and I'll have Henry roll out another container."

Spence accepted bag after bag, dropping them into the cockpit.

Erin watched the interplay, bouncing the baby on her hip. She wasn't sure if she should help unload the bags.

Spence made the choice for her. Dropping the last bag, he reached for the baby.

"Come here, Miranda," he said, his arms outstretched.

Erin handed him the baby and turned towards the young mother. "By the way, I'm Erin Andersen. You have a beautiful daughter."

Suzy smiled in return. Erin wondered if she had seen many women with Spence. It aggravated her that she would now be lumped in the same category as the beautiful actresses and models he dated. On second thought, being mistaken for an actress wasn't so bad, she thought.

"Nice to meet you, Erin. I'm Susan Riger. Have a pleasant voyage and fair winds." She turned to Spence. "Did you file a float plan?"

"Yes, last night. Thanks, Suzy. Tell Mom I'll call her later." He gave Miranda a noisy kiss then blew a loud raspberry on her tummy. The baby squirmed and squealed with delight. Then he handed her to her mother.

"Ewww, she's all slobbery now," Suzy said, using her shirt to wipe off her daughter's tummy. Then she cradled the baby in front of her, waving its tiny hand toward Spence and Erin. "Say 'bye bye.'" Then she walked away, pulling her wagon, her baby cradled on her hip.

Erin watched her retreating back, then turned to Spence. "Thanks for the introduction."

He frowned. "Oh hey, I'm sorry. That's Suzy. She and Henry run the chandlery here at the marina."

"Your manners are appalling," she said, lifting her chin. Righteous indignation flashed in her eyes.

He studied her for a moment before nodding. "You're right. I apologize." He picked up several grocery sacks and handed her one. "Help me stow this food." He paused, then added, "Please."

Erin accepted the bags and followed him into the saloon. She forgot her irritation and turned in a circle, admiring the plush and roomy interior. "My goodness, this is amazing. There's so much space in here."

Spence smiled as he dropped the bags on the galley counter. "Yeah, cats are much more spacious than a single hull sailboat. I'll give you a tour if you stow the groceries."

"Here's the refrigerator," he said. Erin leaned over his arm as he lifted a concealed door.

"Its top loading, so don't put anything you want at the bottom or you won't be able to reach it easily." He dropped the heavy door, then pointed out various drawers. "Here's the pantry. Here's the stove. It's gas, so it cooks quickly. Here's the convection microwave, the dishwasher, and the trash compactor, and over here is a drop-down TV for when you're cooking."

"This is more luxurious than my own kitchen," Erin admired, running her hand across the dark faux stone countertop. Everything was color coordinated and the fixtures were brushed nickel. "Of course, my apartment didn't cost me a million, either."

Spence pointed toward the bow. "My stateroom is forward. Your berth is to port." He picked up her canvas tote and walked down three steps into the port hull.

Erin followed. "This is amazing," she marveled. "I can't believe how big it is. You can't tell from outside that there's this much space."

Spence tossed the tote onto a queen-sized island berth. He opened a small door and tilted his head. "Here's a hanging locker, but there's not a lot of room in it. I keep my stuff in drawers."

He tried to pass Erin, but hesitated in the narrow opening. He put a hand on the bulkhead while he moved around her. At the same time, she stepped out of the way. The end result was her head bumping his chin.

"Oof," he said.

"Ouch," she said, the contact making her bite the inside of her mouth. She touched her tongue pulling away bright red fingertips. "Ecch. I'm bleeding."

"Guess it's not as roomy as you thought, huh?" Spence

said.

"Gueff not," she replied, sticking her tongue out and crossing her eyes at it.

Spence put both hands on her shoulders and turned her in a circle until she faced the head. "Go wash off your tongue. I have to start the blower on the engines."

He bounded up the steps and out the cabin door, moving into the cockpit. She stepped into the head and looked in the mirror, wiggling her tongue around. Nothing serious, she surmised.

She spent several minutes in the head, admiring the vanity, noting the clear-glass shower door and puzzling over the marine toilet. She experimented with the handles and plungers, following the brief directions printed on the side of the contraption.

Satisfied that she could flush it, she went back into the narrow passage and walked towards the bow of the massive catamaran.

The entire width of the boat was dedicated to the owner. She caressed the ultra suede couch then admired the desk in the small office area, complete with a laptop and small entertainment system. She pulled out the wooden tray beneath the desk. It was littered with pens, a watch, keys, a rabbit's foot and some loose change. She stepped into his bathroom, spacious compared to the head she was to use. Still, the fixtures were identical and lavish. She opened the roomy shower door and stepped inside, wondering if she should finagle a way to use his instead of hers. She stepped out of the head and walked toward the huge berth, opening doors and drawers as she explored. The beech wood made for a light and airy compartment, its satiny finish glowing in the filtered light.

A blue comforter covered the king-sized island bed, along with soft pillows. Dog-eared paperback novels sat on a shelf and a pair of worn jeans lay on the cabin sole.

The room smelled like Spence, a mixture of sweat, salt, sunshine and coconut. She shivered, then returned to the galley.

As she unpacked groceries she noted the gourmet supplies and wondered if Spence thought she could cook.

"He's got another think coming," she murmured to herself.

In one cabinet, she saw several bottles of wine, along with bottles of whiskey, bourbon, rum, vodka and tequila. He is prepared for a party, she thought.

She admired the efficiency and compactness of the sailboat; everything had a special place and was bright and clean. Even the garbage can had its own cabinet, the plastic bin lined with a trash bag.

Spence walked into the cabin and began turning on small fans and opening hatches, circulating the fresh air. "We're going to motor out and then raise the sails when we get in open water," he said.

Not sure how to respond, she asked, "Do you need any help?"

"I'll let you know when," he said with an indulgent smile. "I've got the lines arranged for single-handed sailing, so it's efficient."

Stepping over to the navigation center, he flipped on the VHF radio and tuned in to Channel 16. He listened for a minute, then turned the volume down and went back into the cockpit. Erin heard a grinding as the twin diesel engines started.

"Erin, can you cast off the bow line?"

"Sure." She came out of the cabin and stepped onto the port hull, marveling at the wide, slip-resistant path. Nervous, she held the lifelines as she made her way forward. She inched past the large trampoline spanning the two hulls near the catamaran's bow. The stretchy mesh fabric served as a lightweight deck, making it possible to go from one hull to the other without having to return to the cockpit. She stifled an urge to bounce on it before she made her way to the pulpit seat. She sat first, then leaned over and lifted the line, tugging on it to pull the boat closer to the pier. She slid the line up and over the pole, then dropped it in a small pile and walked aft. Spence had already released the stern and the spring lines and was sitting at the helm, one hand on the massive wheel and the other on the throttle.

"Ready?" He smiled.

"Aye, aye." She moved to the back of the cockpit and sat on one of the blue seat cushions. A hardtop canopy shaded the back of the boat. She couldn't see his eyes behind his polarized sunglasses.

He slipped the engines into gear and the massive sailboat powered away from the pier.

Erin leaned back, excitement building in the pit of her stomach. She studied Spence as he manipulated the large steering wheel, occasionally looking over his shoulder as he angled the huge catamaran away from the piers. A breeze lifted wavy hair away from his face and flapped his open shirt. He stood, studying the bridge deck, calculating the distance he needed to clear a moored fishing boat.

Overhead, seagulls wheeled, their raucous calls lifting her spirits higher. A sedate, brown pelican, his bill tucked under his wing, raised his head to watch as "Fusion" slipped from the harbor.

After a few minutes, Spence glanced over his shoulder. "You still here?"

"Of course," Erin said, her eyes closed in bliss. She'd sailed before, and a boat was a boat. This was a floating palace.

"You're so quiet; I thought maybe you jumped ship."

"Not a chance. This is wonderful."

"Can you take the wheel?"

Erin shot up. "What? Why?"

"I need to raise the mainsail."

"I thought you said this was single-handed sailing," Erin said, eyeing the wheel with alarm.

"Well, it is once I get the sail up. The sails are all self-furling with electric winches," he said, "but I need to stow some gear and lines. You want to raise it?"

"No. I'll steer. Where are we going?"

"See the compass? The heading is 125 degrees. Just keep it on this course. I'll be right back. Shout if you see any other boats that might cross our course."

She slipped into the seat and rested her hands on the large wheel. The helm was high and wide and fronted by dials and computer screens filled with nautical charts. The stainless steel throttle vibrated slightly. The compass swung in its binnacle. The heading was southeast, she noted. There was little movement, the twin hulls keeping the boat stable.

Erin took a deep breath. She felt a flutter in the pit of her stomach. I am not afraid, she thought. It's like driving a car. A big car.

Spence took off his shirt and tossed it in a corner of the cockpit. He stepped nimbly onto the cabin roof and checked the mast and boom. He pressed a button and the mainsail pulled out of the mast, sliding along the boom. Soon, the large, white sail slapped resounding as it luffed in the wind.

Erin kept her eyes fastened on the compass, trying not to make jerky movements with the wheel.

Spence checked all the sheets, making sure the cam cleats were in working order. He coiled the bow line that Erin had left in a puddle. He pulled the large, cylindrical fenders aboard and stowed them in a cavernous locker in the port hull. Then he checked the windlass and anchor, making sure the rode was secure.

Satisfied with his brief inspection, he returned to the cockpit and opened a cooler. He withdrew two sodas, popped the tabs and handed one to Erin. She thanked him and sipped the cold beverage while keeping one hand on the wheel. Spence, his head tossed back, his Adam's apple bobbing, emptied the can in several gulps then looked around.

"I forgot to put a trash bag out here." He lifted a locker

lid and tossed the can inside. "Remind me to clean that out, would you?"

Then he came behind Erin and draped an arm over her shoulder. She flinched at the easy familiarity, and jumped from the seat.

"Okay, she's all yours."

Spence grunted and slid behind the wheel. He picked up the exterior VHF radio, adjusted the volume and clicked the handle.

"Suzy-Q, this is "Fusion. You there?" he spoke into the microphone.

Seconds later, Suzy was on the air.

"Yes, Fusion, I'm here. Switch to Channel 9; over."

"Roger that. Moving to Channel 9." Spence depressed a button and the VHF switched channels. The he clicked the hand-held microphone. "Suzy-Q, Fusion here. How about a radio check? Over."

"Fusion, You're loud and clear. How is she? Over."

"She's beautiful. The boat's not bad either," he joked. "Tell Henry we've got plenty of propane. We're leaving the harbor now and heading for open water. Over."

"Not using the Intracoastal Waterway, eh?"

"Nah, we'll make better time sliding down the coastline. The weather forecast is great, so no worries. Can you tell Mom I'll call her later?"

"Will do. Fair winds, Fusion. Suzy out," she replied, signing off.

Checking the navigation system, Spence keyed through the GPS, checking its readout. Then he pressed several buttons on his chart plotter and loaded a map into the autopilot. He reviewed the new chart and calculated the day's passage.

Erin walked into the cabin, not wanting to sit and stare at his broad, muscled back and shoulders. No, that's not right. She did want to stare; she just didn't want him to know it. She had a job to do, and this appeared to be her only option to get it done. "I'm hungry. We missed lunch today. You mind if I find us something to eat?"

"That's a great idea. You can be the chef on this trip."

"Eh, Spence, that's not a good idea. I'll do what I can, but I won't make any promises. I don't even know what capers are for," she said, thinking of the gourmet food they had stowed in the galley cabinets. "I was thinking of a bagel and a cup of coffee."

"Sounds good to me, honey. I'll eat anything."

"Fine. And don't call me honey," she mumbled, stepping into the bright saloon. She pulled a bag of deli fresh bagels from a cabinet.

"Hey! Where's your toaster?"

"Don't have one, babe. Use the oven."

"Oven? You mean the microwave?" she called from inside. "And don't call me babe, either."

"No; use the regular oven."

Erin eyed the propane gas stove and the small oven beneath it mistrustfully, wondering how to light it. She heard a whirl as Spence unfurled the jib. Glancing out the forward port lights, she saw the brilliant blue-and-white sail expand and curve with wind. The catamaran picked up speed and the shore receded. She marveled at the steady motion.

She found a small knife in a drawer and two plates in another cabinet. She sliced the bagels and set them, face up, on the wire rack inside the oven. Then she opened the refrigerator, lifting the large door and leaning inside. She foundered, her feet dangling off of the floor as she scrounged for cream cheese. She knew she had put it inside only twenty minutes earlier.

Spence, hearing her muffled curses, leaned over and looked through the cockpit door. He enjoyed the sight of Erin's bottom wiggling, her bare feet scraping the cabinet doors seeking purchase.

"I told you not to bury anything you wanted," he warned.

"Here it is," she said, standing finally, the cream cheese

in her hand. "From now on, that's your job."

As the bagels toasted, she foraged for coffee beans.

"Dang it! Why did I put them in the refrigerator?" she exclaimed, once again diving head-first into the deep locker. "From now on, they stay on the counter," she said, smoothing back her hair.

She filled the urn with water, experimenting with the foot pump.

"Don't use the foot pump on the right," Spence called out. "That's sea water. Use the one on the left."

She sniffed the water in the urn and crinkled her nose. "Thanks for the warning," she said, pouring it down the drain. She rinsed it several times with fresh water, then filled the coffee machine.

"Don't forget the oven," Spence chimed.

Erin swore again and opened the oven. The bagels had browned and were beginning to singe. She grabbed one and tossed it on the plate, hissing and shaking her burning fingers. "Ouch, ouch," She said as she removed the other bagel. She slammed the oven door and turned off the gas.

She overfilled the coffeepot water and it leaked dark liquid on the counter. Frantic, Erin searched for a washcloth, but couldn't find one. She ran outside and grabbed Spence's discarded shirt and mopped up the coffee.

"Is everything all right, babe?"

"Fine. And quit calling me babe!"

She tossed the soggy, stained shirt into the kitchen sink and leaned against the counter. It's not that difficult to make coffee and bagels she thought. Why am I making such a mess of things?

After a deep breath, she scraped the black edges of the bagels then spread them with cream cheese. She found a couple of mugs in an overhead cabinet and filled them with fresh-brewed coffee. She found sugar in the pantry and half-and-half in the now-hated refrigerator. She put the coffee and bagels and a couple of bananas on a tray and carried it outside wearing, she hoped, a serene smile.

"I don't care how you drink your coffee, Spence. You get cream and sugar today."

"Just the way I like it, honey."

CHAPTER EIGHT

After a dinner of lukewarm tomato soup and ham sandwiches, Spence put the boat on autopilot and opened a bottle of wine. Filling a goblet half way, he handed it to Erin. "You really don't cook, do you?"

"I warned you," she said, stung. "I can make some things. Steak. Salad. Bread."

"You can make bread?"

"Well, I can toast it. Sometimes," she amended, taking the wine from him and raising the glass to her lips. She sighed.

She turned her head to the West, watching out the large windows as the last ray of the sun slipped beneath purple clouds. All day, she watched the starboard shore as they hugged the coastline. Now it was colluded with the setting sun.

"Let's go forward," Spence suggested, breaking her reverie.

Erin followed Spence out of the cabin, walking with care along the hull toward the trampoline. He placed his glass and the bottle on top of a locker and stepped onto the springy tarp. Erin had wanted to walk on the trampoline all day, but was afraid of the open mesh and its proximity to the ocean.

"It won't break, will it?"

"It's safe. Come on; let's watch the stars come out."

Spence opened another forward locker and pulled out two pillows, which he tossed onto the trampoline. Then he stretched out, his head cushioned, his glass cradled on his bare stomach. It reminded Erin of his hammock.

She handed him her wine glass, then stepped onto the trampoline, making him roll. He lifted the glasses to save the deep red liquid from spilling.

"Oops, sorry." She sat and crossed her legs.

He handed her the glass, tapped his against it and said, "To Fusion."

"Confusion," Erin quipped.

"Huh?"

"Never mind. Bad joke."

Standing next to Spence did confuse her. She could feel his body heat, he was so close. And, his scent overwhelmed her.

"What's that fragrance you're wearing?" she asked.

He chuckled. "Men don't wear 'fragrance,' babe. They wear cologne. That would be sweat and maybe a touch of diesel fuel. What you're saying is I stink."

Erin shook her head slightly, his gentle humor relieving a bit of her discomfort. "No, you don't stink. And don't call me 'babe'."

"That bothers you, doesn't it?"

Erin didn't answer. Did it bother her, or was it something else?

"It's important that you remember we're not on vacation. We need to keep a working relationship."

"Relationship? You said you'd get a puppy if you wanted a relationship."

With a severe expression she said, "Spence, there are many types of relationships. The one I'm speaking about now is respect between two people who are ...." She stopped speaking when he grabbed her knee.

"A meteor shower!" He pointed skyward and, wrapping his hand around her wrist, pulled her to the trampoline beside him. "Watch. There at nine o'clock."

Erin did as she was told, her mouth open in surprise, her eyes wide and searching. Then she gasped. "I see one," she said, pointing with glee. "Oh my, I've never seen so many stars. They seem so close."

They remained on the bridge deck, sipping wine and watching stars for another hour before Spence said they were nearing their destination for the night.

"We don't sail through the night?" Erin asked.

"No. Not unless you want to stay up all night and keep watch. We're not in a hurry; you only sail at night when you're making passage. I set the autopilot and we've been heading for a small harbor I know. We'll be there soon and set the anchor."

"Do you need help? What should I do?"

"I'll need you when we take down the sails and set the anchor."

"Okay," she said hesitantly. "Tell me what to do, though. I've only sailed small dinghies, remember?"

He patted her knee. "Don't worry. By the time we're done, you'll be able to handle this boat all by yourself."

"I don't think so, but thanks for the vote of confidence."

She handed him her empty wine glass then stood up. She swayed a bit in the webbing, then grabbed the wire rigging for support. Spence watched from his position on the trampoline, admiring her tanned legs and the small indentations made by the web.

He followed her to the cockpit and checked the chart plotter. He turned off the autopilot, steering a course towards the dark coastline. Soon he turned on the diesel engines. "Keep its nose into the wind while I lower the sails," he said, stepping away from the wheel.

"Where's the wind?"

"I've got it pointed into the wind already, but you see

79

those little strips of yarn on the rigging? Those are tell-tales. They tell you which way the wind is blowing. Just keep your course steady and your eye on the tell-tales. They should be flapping toward the stern of the boat."

"Okay." Recalling the basics of wind direction from sailing dinghies on the lake, she hiked up onto the seat, resting her hands on the wheel.

Spence went forward and furled the jib, tucking the sheets into cam cleats and tying new stopper knots. Then he pressed a button and the mainsail furled into the mast. He checked that all the other lines led back to the helm or were coiled on the deck.

"Put her in neutral," he called to Erin.

She looked at the two-lever throttle control.

"Which one do I use?" She yelled.

"Both," Spence replied loudly. "They operate both the port and starboard engines."

She slid the handles into neutral, then stood on the chair's footrest to see over the cabin roof. She could see Spence bend over the bow, an anchor held lightly in one hand and its chain in the other. He dropped the heavy steel plow anchor into the water, paying out the chain rode, then the line attached to it. She heard the motor whirl of the electric windlass. He stood and checked to make sure no other boats were nearby. "Put her in reverse. Go slow."

Erin slid the handles into reverse. The sound of the big diesel engines changed as they slipped from neutral into reverse.

Spence watched the anchor line then held up a fist. "Okay, stop."

She put the controls back into neutral.

Spence knelt on the bridge deck and tugged on the line that led into the ocean. "One more time. Back up slowly, then stop."

Erin did as he asked, repeating the process twice more before Spence was satisfied that the anchor was set. He tied a bridle leading from the port and starboard hulls onto the anchor rode after sliding a heavy, lead kedge down the line. "That should keep us from sashaying tonight," he said.

Returning to the cockpit, he turned off the engines and set the GPS anchor alarm. If the boat moved more than usual as it swung on the anchor, then the crew would be alerted. No captain wanted to sleep through the predicament of a dragging anchor.

Erin moved from the helm to the cockpit door.

"It's late. I guess I'll get ready for bed."

Spence nodded, still reviewing his navigation screens.

"I'll wrap things up here. You head on in."

She went down in to the port hull and gathered her bath supplies. She took a quick, cramped shower, then dressed in a T-shirt and pair of panties. She'd packed quickly and under pressure, leaving most of her clothes at Spence's house. She didn't even pack a bra.

After she had curled in the berth, she realized she had nothing to read. She tucked the quilt around her and called out.

"Spence? Are you there?"

"Yes," he said, his head and shoulders appearing in the passageway. "Are you all right?"

"Yes. But I need something to read. I didn't pack anything except my laptop and I've left it in the saloon. Can you bring it to me?"

"Sure." He reappeared with her briefcase. "Are you sure you're all right?"

"I'm sure. I don't have many clothes on, and I don't want to parade around your boat half-dressed. Thank you," she said primly, taking the briefcase and unzipping it. She flipped open the screen and looked at him. "Thank you," she repeated.

"You're welcome," he said, a wicked grin on his face. He flopped beside her and tugged at her quilt. "You don't have any clothes on?"

"I said I don't have 'many' clothes on. Of course I'm

wearing clothes. Now get out of here." She kicked at him, a feeble effort under the fluffy spread.

"Whatcha working on?" he persisted, stroking her covered knee.

"Go away," she said between clenched teeth. "You're dismissed. Shoo."

"I thought you wanted to work on the book. Isn't that what you're being paid to do?"

"Yes, I am," she retorted. "But not at night and in my bed. Quit teasing me, Spence."

His gaze settled on her breasts and as if magnetized, he raised a hand towards them. Then he glanced into her face, noted her red-stained cheeks and brilliant eyes and decided to retreat.

"Babe, I would never tease you," he drawled, dropping his hand. "Good night. If you need anything, just yell."

He was gone. Erin couldn't hear his footsteps; her heart was pounding and blood roared in her ears. She didn't know if she should be angry or frightened, then she realized she was neither. She was excited and a flame licked through her chest. She wanted Spence to touch her, to stroke her breast the way he stroked her knee. She hid her face in her hands, blotting out a vision of him lying on her bed. Her computer slid off of her lap, unnoticed.

CHAPTER NINE

Erin found life aboard the catamaran comfortable. She didn't mind the close quarters and loved lounging in the wide cockpit while Spence handled the ship's wheel. She worked on her tan, wearing her bathing suit top and a pair of shorts. Spence wore a pair of trunks and his ever-present sunglasses. Behind her own sunglasses, Erin watched as he steered with little effort, adjusting the sheets and the sails from controls near his seat. Each morning, he turned on the autopilot and set a line, trolling for fish. On occasion, he caught something that he had to clean, cook, and eat alone.

Spence discovered that Erin was much better with the navigation charts and plotting a course than sautéing or baking. It amused him that she didn't bother to try to cook for him, unlike other women he had dated. Often, they tried to impress him with their domestic skills. Erin didn't bother.

They talked; she asked him about his family, his childhood and how he became an artist. Spence answered all of her questions, but he didn't pry. Still, she chatted about herself. In the evening, as agreed, they worked on his book. Erin felt triumphant after they finished the introduction.

"I'm glad it makes you happy," he said.

"Of course it does. It should please you, as well. I'm proud of you."

He laughed at her enthusiasm. "They teach you positive reinforcement at grad school?"

"No. It comes from years of working with lazy, selfish artists who only think of themselves."

"Hey, I didn't volunteer for this."

"You signed a contract. You accepted the advance. You had a clue that a book is the end result."

* * *

On their fourth day out, Erin felt confident enough to raise the anchor. "I am so glad you have a fancy electric winch for this anchor," she said.

"Manual labor's good for you, but hoisting an anchor isn't," Spence replied, a cigar clenched between his teeth.

"Must you smoke that smelly thing?"

"Yeah. It's a vice. You want to try one?"

"No, ick." She moved away from him, waving a hand in the air as if it were thick with smoke. In truth, she was getting used to the aromatic tobacco he used but she appreciated the fact that he smoked only one a day.

He tossed her a bottle. "Hey babe; how about some sunscreen?"

"I told you not to call me babe," she said, aggravation causing frown lines. She squirted white cream into her hands and began to stroke them up and down her arms, then her legs.

"I meant me," he complained.

"I know. Give me a minute."

He watched covertly as she squirted more into her hands and rubbed them on her belly and her breasts, sliding her fingers under her bikini top and straps.

"You want me to do your back?"

"Yes. You do me; I'll do you," she said, handing him the bottle and turning her back to him.

Spence swiveled and leaned back in the wide captain's seat. He tossed his cigar into waves and squirted sunscreen into his large, calloused hands.

His touch, rough and warm, startled Erin. He slid his big fingers over her shoulders, up her neck and rubbed her ears. "Don't want those to burn," he murmured. Then his hands returned, slathered with more lotion, and he ran them up and down her back, making small circles on her spine, sliding them around her waist. He slid his fingers into the loose elastic waistband of her shorts and pushed them down a few inches. Then he rubbed lotion on her lower back, his hands spreading and wrapping around her hips, cupping them. Erin tried to ignore the rapid beat of her heart, the tickling sensations of his warm hands.

"That's good," she said, pulling away. "Now you. Turn around."

Spence blotted his hands on a towel while he checked the autopilot then took off his faded ball cap and tossed it on the cockpit table.

"Do my face and ears, please." He removed his sunglasses and closed his eyes.

"You can do that yourself."

"No. You do it. I've wiped off my hands. I don't want to get the controls greasy."

Erin bit her lip. "Sounds like an excuse to me. You're just lazy."

"No; you're better than me. You get all the right spots."

"You want to be pampered."

Spence smiled, his eyes still closed. "I'll make something special for dinner tonight," he bargained.

Erin squirted a little lotion into her hands, rubbed them together and started applying it in small quick motions to his cheeks and ears. He turned his face into her hands like a dog angling for a scratch. She smiled and traced his stubbled chin, his broad forehead, his nose. "You need some zinc here," she said.

She shook the bottle and squirted more into her hands. She placed them on his shoulders, rubbing up and down the thick cords of his neck, then to the furry center of his bare chest.

"Why do you wear this," she asked, shoving her fingers under the ubiquitous St. Christopher's medal.

"It was my father's. My mother got it for him when they took a second honeymoon in Hawaii."

"Oh." Why did he have to be sentimental? Every day he became a bit more appealing. It was most unnerving, especially when she was touching his warm skin. For a moment, she fantasized about leaning in and kissing his parted lips, burying her face into his neck and inhaling the sweet coconut scent of the lotion. Instead, she picked up the bottle of sunscreen, squirted some into her hand.

"This is empty," she said, running her hands along his right arm.

Spence put his sunglasses back on. "There's another bottle in the port locker."

She opened the trash locker and added the empty bottle to the growing pile of crushed soda cans and water bottles. Then she reached into the port locker, pushing aside bags of snorkel equipment and life preservers. Indeed, there was a case of sunscreen, the cardboard box ripped open. There were still a couple dozen bottles. "Why do you have so many?"

"It's easier. Suzy includes me when she orders bulk supplies."

"Humph. I suppose you go through a lot of this what with the models and actresses?" Erin wanted to toss the bottle at his head.

"Not me, babe," he said. "You're the first female to board this boat."

"Right," she drawled sarcastically. "Like I believe that. And don't call me babe," she huffed as she opened the new bottle. She lifted his left arm and squirted a thick line from his wrist to his bicep. She rubbed it in and then, wiping the excess lotion on her shorts bottom, turned the chair so Spence was facing the ocean. She squirted more than she needed on his back, spelling the word "jerk."

She slapped his back a couple of times and tossed the bottle onto the cockpit table. "Okay, all done."

"Aw, come on, Erin. You haven't finished my back. I'll get burned." He wheedled, "I'm making dinner, remember? You want me to grill steaks?"

She stared at the boat's wake, biting her lip. Why was she so angry? It was unreasonable, she knew, for her to feel nervous when close to him, or threatened by a thought of other women aboard his boat.

She stepped forward and rubbed the rest of the lotion into his skin. "There. Now you're done. And I want mushrooms and onions on my steak."

Spence watched as she picked up a beach towel and tote bag and headed for the bow of the boat. She spread the towel on the trampoline, pulled a visor and glasses out of the bag, and laid on her stomach, her head resting on her crossed arms.

He would never understand women, he thought, craving his cigar. One minute they're fine, the next they're not.

CHAPTER TEN

Six days into the passage, Spence pointed towards the coastline. "There's St. Augustine."

Erin shaded her eyes and followed his pointing finger. In the distance she could see bumps on the western horizon.

"Are we stopping there?"

"Would you like to?"

"Yes. I think I'm going stir crazy, looking at your goofy face all day. I need to see other people."

Spence smiled. "Goofy? Well, at least I'm not a sour puss."

"I'm not a sour puss. I need to walk around on dry land. And I could use some things. We left so quickly, I left a lot behind."

"That's the point, sweetheart. Travel light."

"Well, there are some things a woman needs. And right now, chocolate is one of them."

Spence nodded wisely. "Ah yes. Things a woman needs. Can do."

Spence and Erin were not a well-oiled team, still three hours later they managed to drop the sails and motor into the St. Augustine Municipal Marina. A quick call on the

VHF reserved the huge catamaran an outside slip, making it easy and convenient to dock.

After helping to secure Fusion to the pier, Erin grabbed her purse and headed for the marina's chandlery. Spence checked all of the through-hull fittings for leaks and, finding none, he turned off the power. They agreed to meet at the front of the marina. The sun would be setting within an hour, so they would have time to walk the neighborhood and find a restaurant.

Erin was fidgeting by the time he arrived at the marina store. "Come on. Hurry up."

Spence took her hand. "What's your hurry?"

She tried to tug her hand free. He held it tighter.

"I want to look around before its dark." She lifted her chin and sniffed. "Do you smell that?"

"What?"

"Trash. Exhaust fumes. People."

"You like that?" He shook his head in wonder.

"No, not really but I miss it. Remember, I live in the city."

They strolled towards the historic district, admiring the Spanish architecture. Dozens of small shops lined the streets, many with tables arranged outdoors. Erin stopped to admire the preserved alligator heads, carved coconut faces, postcards and citrus-themed snow globes.

They walked past several restaurants until Erin froze in front of The Columbia. She inhaled the exotic aromas of the famous Spanish restaurant, then pulled Spence inside.

"Hello. Dinner for two? Do you have reservations?" A lovely, dark-haired young hostess greeted them as they walked in the plush restaurant.

"Two, please. No, we don't have reservations." Spence smiled, offering his hand to the hostess. She smiled in return.

"One moment; let me check." She consulted a chart on her podium, then made a mark and picked up two menus. "Follow me, please."

She ushered Spence and Erin past a row of people also waiting for tables. Erin avoided their faces, feeling a bit guilty that Spence's sex appeal meant prompt seating. Once at the table, however, she shed her remorse, read the menu and began to salivate.

After a waiter took their drink order, Erin glanced over the top of her menu at Spence. "What are you getting?"

"I'm not sure."

"Want to share an appetizer? Maybe two?"

Spence frowned. "What you are thinking?"

"Well, I'm going to order the Queso Fundido. Mmmm, warm cheese and toasty Cuban bread. But I also want the empanadas. The beefy turnovers with salsa."

"I'll consider sharing if we can add the jumbo chilled shrimp."

"You've got a deal."

For her entrée, Erin ordered the house special, a broiled center-cut filet mignon. Spence asked for the red snapper.

"Excellent choice, sir. That recipe was created by the owner's grandfather many years ago. It comes with our highest recommendation." The waiter filled his tablet and scurried away.

Erin sipped the fruity sangria wine Spence had chosen, closing her eyes. "This is decadent. It's exactly what I needed. Sorry, I'm not much of a sailor, am I?"

"It's your first voyage. It's like camping out. You have to get used to doing without a lot of amenities."

"Hah! That's a floating palace. You've even got a washing machine that will dry clothes also, for God's sake. You've got TV, the Internet and satellite radio. You even have gallons of sunscreen so the babes can oil you down. You're not suffering."

"I didn't say I was suffering. I enjoy sailing and I like my toys. You want me to apologize?"

Erin rolled her eyes and took another sip. She wondered if she was becoming one of his "toys."

"What's the problem? Why are you angry? Did I offend you?"

She shook her head stubbornly. "No. I'm not upset."

"Are you sure? Is there anything I can do?"

She pounced. "Yes, there is. You can buckle down and get to work on the book. You've been wasting too much time the past two days fishing."

"Fishing? Trolling a line isn't fishing. And it doesn't waste time. I eat what I catch, don't I?"

"I don't eat fish, so it isn't making my life convenient."

"Ah, I understand now. You've been eating your own cooking this week and you don't like it."

He wouldn't understand, Erin thought. She didn't even understand. During the past few days, she had struggled with the fact that she was attracted to him. Yet he seemed impervious. Sure, he was considerate and easy going and he always used endearments when he talked to her. But to a man like Stephen Spence, every woman was a "babe" or a "honey."

"I needed a night out. Some not-so-fresh air, I guess."

The dinner ended too soon, she thought, but they took their time walking downtown before heading back to the marina. As the night deepened, people filled the streets. Doors to taverns were opened, beckoning them. They stopped at a noisy bar and Spence ordered them both mojitos.

"This is delicious," Erin exclaimed. "What's in it?"

The young bartender leaned on the mahogany counter, admiring Erin. "It's a combination of rum, simple sugar, mint and soda." He grinned, his teeth bright in the dim bar.

Erin smiled at the handsome man. "It's wonderful."

"It's on the house, pretty lady," he replied, winking at her.

She thanked him and smirked at Spence.

Spence smiled good-naturedly. He understood perfectly well.

She considered her flirtation with the bartender as tit-for-tat for the Columbia's hostess. Obviously, she hadn't seen the twenty he had palmed and handed to the young woman at the restaurant. He tipped the bartender generously when they departed.

Back aboard the boat, Erin put her leftovers in the refrigerator and said good night. With a large hot water heater and its own water maker, Fusion's shower was a refuge from her conflicting emotions.

As she crawled beneath the soft comforter, the boat rocking gently, Erin hugged her pillow to her chest. In the dark, she found it easy to let her mind wander. To imagine Spence sleeping in his berth on the far side of the boat. She allowed herself to fantasize about how it would feel to rest her head against him. She hiked her pillow up until it felt like a warm shoulder, closed her eyes and smiled.

CHAPTER ELEVEN

"I'm thinking a couple days in Key West might be fun. Ever been there?"

"No. My parents live in Sarasota, though."

"Would you like to go there? See them?"

"You're kidding, right?"

"We can go to the Tortugas first. We'll do a little snorkeling and tour Fort Jefferson. It's an old Civil War fort. Very cool. Then take a side trip to the Gulf Coast."

"Isn't that fort way past Key West?"

"Nah, it's not too far. This cat is fast and I'm in no hurry. The weather's great and there aren't any storms on the radar."

She shivered. "That's good."

"Don't let a little weather worry you. This boat is blue-water certified."

"What does that mean?"

Spence squinted at the compass, then adjusted the autopilot. "It means I can sail her anywhere I want. How about the South Pacific?"

"You jest," Erin said. "No; I think Key West is tropical enough for me."

"Want me to add Sarasota as a waypoint? Want me to

meet the parents?"

"Thank you, no. I'm working, remember? We're both working. I'll see my parents at Christmas."

* * *

Later that evening, Erin e-mailed two chapters and essays on a dozen paintings to Patricia's office. She also uploaded digital copies of Spence's paintings along with detailed captions.

She was excited that work on the book was progressing, albeit slowly, and that Spence liked her outline. She resorted to interviewing him and then transcribing tapes and notes into a first-person format. The thoughts and feelings were his and they were real; she was simply the conduit for getting those thoughts on paper.

"You're good at this, aren't you?"

Erin glowed at the compliment. "I enjoy working with writers. I love being an editor."

"Why don't you write your own book?"

"Don't be silly."

"Why not? I mean, why not write your own book? Why do you want to work with other people when you could just do what you want?"

"Spence, this is what I want to do. I'm happy working with talented people and helping them create a new piece of art. That's what a book is, of course. As an artist, your goal is to produce a painting, not a book. But with my help, you can build a bridge between painting and writing."

She could tell he still didn't understand.

"All right, think of me as the conductor of a symphonic orchestra. I'm not playing the instruments; I'm directing those who can. With my guidance, we create a work of art. Sure, I know how to write, like the conductor knows how to read music and play instruments. But with his help, the musicians create the magic."

Spence shrugged, not agreeing. "If you say so. Seems like you should be getting the credit, though."

"Believe me; I am paid well to stay in the background. I don't require my name on the cover. I'm not an ego maniac. I get satisfaction from doing my job well. From knowing that my employer is satisfied and that I have helped a new author produce a quality book."

"I'm not an ego maniac," he retorted.

"I didn't say you were. Sheesh."

"Okay, you're not an ego maniac. You're a control freak."

"I am not!" She tried to shove him out of the settee, using her hands and then her feet for advantage. Spence grabbed her ankles and tickled her toes.

"So how much do you make on a book like this?"

"None of your business, smarty pants."

"Seriously," he said.

"Well, not a half million, that's for sure. How much do you make on a single painting?"

Spence grinned and rubbed his hands, pantomiming a greedy miser. "Wouldn't you like to know?"

"Actually, I already know."

"Well why'd ya ask?"

"To see if you'd tell me the truth."

"I see. You're testing me. I wondered when you'd start."

She glared at him as she shut her laptop. "Oh, get real. I couldn't care less about testing you. Get out of my way."

She waited for him to move and when he didn't she scooted to the opposite edge of the settee. She was growing frustrated, fighting her conflicting emotions, and resorted to sniping at him. If she didn't keep him at a distance, she might throw herself in his arms.

* * *

By late afternoon, she could see the Tortuga beach and

95

the red brick structure of Fort Jefferson shimmering on the horizon.

"Are there many people on the island?"

"No. The only people who live here are park rangers and their families. It's nice to visit, but it's not hospitable. There's no fresh water–just coral and sand. That's why Spanish sailors called it the 'Dry Tortugas.' Even pirates avoided this place, except when they needed to maroon a kidnapped damsel."

Erin shaded her eyes and watched as the islands drew closer. She read the tattered brochure Spence dug out of the starboard locker. She learned that "Tortuga" is Spanish for turtle and the old brick fort had been built in the 1800s, but never saw any real military action. Its biggest claim to fame came after the Civil War, when it served as a prison. Decades of neglect and the occasional hurricane left parts of the fort crumbling, but the National Park Service was doing its best to stay ahead of the elements. Now, the main island and six lesser keys nearby serve as a remote outpost for small groups of tourists who make the seventy-mile, open-water trip from Key West. Other visitors included the occasional bird-watcher, scientists studying the turtle population, and sailors like Spence.

"Are we going to be here long?"

"Nah. We'll do a little snorkeling and stay tonight. Then tomorrow morning we'll head on to Key West, do a little Duval crawlin', get some Cuban grub."

"What's 'Duval crawling'?"

"You'll see," he said, smirking. "Meanwhile, let's drop anchor at that small mangrove island north of Tortuga. We can take the dinghy to the fort."

"Why don't we head for the piers?" Erin asked, nodding towards a series of dark wooden poles near the shore.

"We're going to stay the night and I don't want company. Sometimes other cruisers come here and they like to party too much. They can be too loud."

"Oh," she said, noticing a small sailboat and a sport fishing boat tied to the piers. In the distance, a commercial ferry was leaving Tortuga and Erin could see the stern was crowded with tourists.

Within minutes they secured the anchor and lowered the inflatable dinghy. Spence helped Erin into the little boat and tossed her a bag of gear and a picnic basket.

"What's this?"

"We'll do a little snorkeling before we go to Fort Jefferson. See some wildlife that the tourists won't see."

He climbed in and started the motor. After days of quiet sailing and the occasional muffled diesel, the roar of the powerful gasoline motor startled her. Spence, sitting at the stern and guiding the tiller, grinned. He pushed the little speedboat and made great, loping circles until Erin laughed, clinging to the inflated sides.

At the beach, Spence tied the Zodiac to the exposed roots of a mangrove. He dumped the contents of the bag into the boat, then handed Erin a mask, snorkel and set of fins. He showed her how to adjust the mask and blow through the snorkel. Then, he helped her with her fins. She waddled to the surf and turned around to wait for him.

"Remember, don't touch," he said as he bent over to rinse his mask in the water. Oh, how she wanted to touch. "Especially the corals. Touching is bad for them, and bad for you if you touch the kind that burns your skin."

They swam several yards out and Spence pointed to a dark patch of water, signifying a coral head. Erin inserted her snorkel and dove under the water. At only ten feet deep, it was easy to see the sandy ocean floor.

She marveled at the silence, broken by the splash of her flippers and her breath through the snorkel. She hovered near a patch of coral, watching as yellow and blue and purple tropical fish darted through the shallow water. She floated toward Spence, her green eyes dancing as she surveyed the underwater paradise.

A large manta ray swam past them, then doubled back.

Frightened, Erin grabbed Spence's arm, pointing before she broke through the surface, sputtering. Spence laughed, then groaned as she scrambled up his body and away from the ray.

Her arms were around his neck, her fins poking him in his stomach.

"What is that? Is it dangerous? Some kind of sting ray?"

"It's a ray but don't worry. It won't harm you," he said, smiling. "They're gentle."

Spence wrapped her legs around his hips, moving her threatening fins away from his groin. He slid one hand around her waist, the other cupped her bottom.

Erin wasn't convinced. She put her chin on his shoulder and stared behind him at the open water. It took him several minutes of stroking her back and talking about the sea life before she let him go. She wasn't sure if she should be embarrassed; Spence acted as if nothing had happened.

For another hour, they explored beds of coral and the colorful fish that lived there. She picked up sand dollars, stuffing them in the side of her bathing suit. She accepted the surroundings, gaining a little confidence.

Soon, they returned to the secluded beach. Spence pulled a colorful blanket from the boat and spread it on the sand, anchoring one corner with the small cooler. Then he sat and pulled two bottles of water and some fruit out of the cooler. During the past week of sailing and eating well, he had dropped some weight. Erin poked him in the stomach.

"How do you do that?"

"Pardon me?"

"How do you lose weight so quickly and where were those abs last week?"

"Ah, you want to know my secret? Each morning I do crunches and I have a set of dumbbells in my cabin. Fifteen minutes of strength training and I'm good to go."

He flexed a bicep and smiled. "Go ahead. I know you want to touch it."

Her mind swam. The sun, the water, the man and this paradise a million miles from anywhere made her feel woozy. She ignored the warning bells. At the moment, danger was far from her thoughts.

Erin squeezed his upper arm and sighed. "Oh, Popeye." Then she took a bite of a peach. Juice dripped down her chin and onto her chest. The smell of ripe fruit blended with salt air. She needed a napkin but was out of luck. She lifted her hand to wipe off her chin but Spence caught it. He leaned forward and sucked at her chin. Then he licked the juice off of her chest. Erin couldn't breathe. He brushed a curl from her forehead and whispered, "You taste as good as you look."

Erin swooned.

In one easy movement, she was on her back and Spence was leaning over her. The forgotten peach rolled from her hand. He brushed her hair from her face and then traced her profile with his finger. He paused at her lips, his thumb caressing them. Erin couldn't tear her eyes from his. Nervous, she opened her mouth and wet her lips. Kiss me. Oh, kiss me, she thought.

He did and he tasted like salt and sugar. Erin closed her eyes and kissed him back. Her arms snaked around his neck and she pressed closer, wanting to feel his chest against hers. Spence reached behind her neck and untied her top. He tugged it down and then held her close, crushing her breasts against him. Erin gasped at the sensation of bare skin.

Once again, Spence captured her mouth and his tongue danced with hers. They kissed for several minutes before Spence pulled away.

"I want to make love to you."

"I know," she whispered.

"You want me, too."

She didn't answer. Spence kissed her chin then her ear.

"Tell me you want me," he commanded.

Still, Erin said nothing. She turned her head away.

"Tell me," he said.

She dropped her arms. "I don't think we should do this."

Smiling at her, he pulled her bikini straps up and tied them behind her neck. He helped her to her feet and wiped sand off of her back. Resting his forearms on her shoulders, he placed his forehead against hers. Looking into her troubled green eyes he said, "Soon."

She blinked.

He kissed her, then ran for the surf. He dove in and caught a wave.

"C'mon. You know how to body surf?"

CHAPTER TWELVE

After rousing Erin in pre-dawn light, Spence weighed anchor and sailed close-hauled to Key West. He radioed ahead for a slip in the historic marina and by late afternoon they closed the hatches and locked the saloon door for a trip to town.

Ashore, they ate at a small Cuban restaurant, washing down the spicy food with bottles of icy beer. Erin kept the conversation light and impersonal.

"So, you've lived in North Carolina all your life?"

Spence leaned back in the bamboo chair, his eyes resting on the harbor. Sailboats were milling about, ferrying tourists on the daily sunset cruises.

"Mostly," he said. "I've been a few other places but North Carolina's home."

"Will you live there from now on?"

Spence took the fork out of her hand and turned it over, tracing her palm with one large finger. "That's the plan."

She closed her hand, making a fist. Spence laughed.

"Relax, babe." At her frown he added, "I mean, Erin."

They talked and laughed and drank too much beer. Erin was giddy with excitement and she couldn't stop blushing. Instead of returning to the boat, Spence had checked them into the adjoining hotel. Soon they were standing outside her room. Erin leaned against the wall as he unlocked the door. He bent to kiss her and she lifted her face in anticipation. Hungry, he sought her neck and throat. Encircling his waist with her arms, she whispered, "Where's your room?"

"Here," he said as door open. He swept her into his arms and, keeping his mouth fastened on hers, kicked the door shut behind them.

The mattress dipped as he laid her gently on the bed. His hands glided over her belly, pushing her T-shirt aside.

"Spence," she whispered.

"Erin," he countered huskily.

"We shouldn't be here."

"Where would you rather be?"

"That's not what I mean."

Spence rolled onto his back, pulling her on top. His hands worked deftly sliding her shirt up and over her head. Rosy nipples hung before his eyes, tantalizing and lush. He asked, "You're a logical woman, aren't you, Erin?"

"Yes," she moaned as his tongue sparred with her breast, brushing lightly across the tense nipple.

"How do you explain the fact that you're here, soon to be naked and in my bed?" He suckled while his fingers pushed her shorts from the small of her back, over her hips and down her legs.

He didn't understand her distress. She felt guilty because she'd been hired to help him. Instead, she skipped aboard his boat, lounged around in a skimpy bathing suit, flirted outrageously and danced provocatively with him. Every day since she had met him, she made it clear she desired him. How could she blame him for wanting her? How could she refuse what he offered?

Instead of pulling away, she settled closer to him, a thin wisp of silk separating her from his low-slung khakis. She rubbed gently against his zipper, moaning softly as the cold, sharp steel bit into her sensitive skin. "You kidnapped me," she whispered as the last of her resistance melted away. "Just like the pirates on Tortuga."

He slid a hand between them, sliding down his zipper. He pulled himself free and rubbed against her. "You want your freedom?"

"No." She gasped at the sensation, unable to stop from squirming. His hand traced small slick circles that she found irresistible.

He moaned softly as she angled herself, capturing his teasing hand with hers and wrapping her fingers around him.

She couldn't keep her hands off of him, couldn't keep her tongue in her mouth. She loved the taste of his skin, had wondered about it for days.

"Why shouldn't we be here?" He shifted his hips and she groaned with pleasure, with torment.

She had no response other than to tug and pull at his clothes until they were in a pile on the floor. Erin wrapped her arms around his neck, her mouth fused to his as he slid inside. Only her panties separated them, and when she touched the waistband to push them down, Spence captured her fingers, loathing the thought of moving apart.

"No; I like them on," he said, rubbing against the silk fabric as he slid in and out. He laughed and splayed his hands across her bottom, first cupping her towards him then lifting her up as his strokes lengthened.

Erin arched her back, seeking that electric sensation. Her breathing grew fast and shallow, and she wanted him to move faster. Instead, Spence captured her hips, pacing her frenzied movements. "Slow down, baby. Not yet," he whispered, his mouth once again fastening on her breast.

Her head sagged as she struggled to separate pleasure and torture. She wanted desperately to move with him, but her body insisted on its own rhythm. Beads of perspiration formed on her upper lip as she concentrated on that sweet, deep tug. Her climax took her by surprise, beginning as a slow, rippling wave. She whimpered at the dizzying force then froze, wanting to hold onto the sweet sensation. She could feel herself flexing and grasping Spence who, with a guttural cry of pleasure, crushed her hips into his.

Exhausted, Erin sank, placing her fevered cheek against his chest. She heard his heart thunder, felt his arms tremble as they wrapped around her and she gloated at her power. She snuggled into him, her possessive arm draped across his waist. She yawned and within moments, lethargy won and she slept.

Spence caressed her in the moonlight. Her blonde hair fell beneath her shoulders, curling over one breast. Her dark eyebrows arched over heavy-lidded eyes that he thought may be closer to emerald than ordinary green. Her nose was straight and small; her lips were soft and curved. Their lovemaking had removed her lipstick, but passion had reddened them and his kisses had left them swollen. He continued his survey, down her neck to the tiny gold chain with a small key charm. He smiled as he recalled her reluctance when he bought it on a whim from a Duval Street art gallery. He insisted she wear it knowing that evening it would be the only thing touching her skin—besides him and the bed sheets.

Her dusky-tipped breasts rose with each breath and his hands ached to touch them. He licked his lips, remembering their fullness and her urgent demands that he suck harder.

She pulled on a sheet after their lovemaking, and it rested on her rounded hip. Her legs, invisible beneath the blanket, were tapered. During the past week, she had developed a golden glow, despite copious amounts of sunscreen.

She is so beautiful, he thought as he drifted to sleep.

CHAPTER THIRTEEN

When Erin awoke, she studied Spence's sleeping profile and frowned. She once again felt embarrassed and shy and tried to slip out of the bed. Without opening his eyes, he caught her wrist and pulled her to him.

"Where are you going?"

She hesitated, unable to answer. When he turned his head and opened his eyes she blushed and stammered.

"Shhh, baby. It's okay." He kissed her gently and tucked her under his arm, pressing her head to his chest. She listened to his heartbeat, steady and slow now. Timidly, she touched him, her fingers making slow sweeps along his abdomen. He caught her hand in his, placed the palm against his lips. A feeling of warmth washed over her and she snuggled against him.

"What do you want to do today?"

Erin had no reply; her mind a blank except for the sensation of his body against hers. She turned her back to him, curling into a ball. He nuzzled the back of her neck and, feeling her shiver, nipped it. Her legs straightened and she found his hands, cupped them under her breasts. She rubbed her bottom against him suggestively.

"Okay. We'll stay in," he said.

Later, they took a shower together and after a light lunch, strolled through the streets of Key West holding hands. She bought a straw hat to keep the sun from burning her nose. They stopped at a boutique and she found a colorful, cotton sundress she liked. He followed her into the changing room and helped her remove it, his hands on her body, his kisses drugging her. He chuckled at her dreamy expression.

"You like that?"

"Yes, I do."

Erin didn't realize it, caught up in her own euphoria, but Spence was enchanted by her every move. He couldn't stop watching her, couldn't keep his hands off of her. Every few minutes he stopped her for a kiss.

She accepted all of his attention without question. Being with Spence was the easiest and the most wonderful thing she had ever done, once she quit resisting.

They spent a week in Key West, exploring, eating, and making love. Each evening at sunset, they stood shoulder-to-shoulder on Mallory Pier and watched the sky melt into hot orange, then brilliant pinks and purples.

They spent one night and late into the next morning on the "Duval Crawl," a favorite pastime of tourists and locals alike. The crawl consisted of barhopping on Duval Street and included famous places like Sloppy Joe's, as well as the not-so-famous, yet still charming, dives. Tequila flows like water in Key West, Erin thought.

They explored Old City, riding scooters and hopping trolleys. He leased a powerboat and took her deep-sea fishing, laughing with joy when she hooked–then lost–a marlin.

When it was time to leave, Erin shuffled several shopping bags into the spare berth. Spence had given a Key West bracelet to match her necklace. She bought herself several new bathing suits, and some interesting lingerie from a specialty store that also catered to the local drag queens.

Erin accepted his two gifts with reluctance, embarrassed by his generosity but craving his smile, his approval. He silenced her protests with his relentless lips and warm, strong hands.

"Not fair, not fair," she murmured one morning as he pulled one of a pair of emerald earrings out of the velvet box and placed it in her belly button.

"They're the same color as your eyes," he whispered, his tongue tracing her inner thigh.

Back on the catamaran, they explored shallow waters and cays where deep-drafted sailboats couldn't venture, and she perfected her tan, without lines. She discovered that she enjoyed lying around nude, while Spence stood at the wheel, his sunglasses on, the breeze whipping through his wavy hair. It was a luxurious life and they agreed to spend another week cruising the Keys.

Finally, Spence turned the cat north. On the voyage home, Erin worked with him on the book, e-mailing McDowell two more chapters. They hadn't kept to her schedule, and Erin found it difficult to keep track of time.

Once the boat was secure in its dock at the Ocracoke marina, Erin tossed her canvas tote bag and her briefcase into the backseat of the SUV. Shopping bags filled the trunk.

Spence lifted the floor mat, picked up the keys and smiled. "Ready to go home?"

Erin thrilled at the words as if it were, indeed, her home. She nodded.

* * *

The first two days at home, Spence worked in his studio. Erin didn't intrude; she understood the artist's method. She spent her time sightseeing, visiting the lighthouses nearby and shopping in the village. She bought groceries and planned meals, tuning into cooking shows for recipes. Some worked, some didn't. Spence gamely ate all, even chili so hot that tears rolled down his cheeks. "What? I love spicy food!" he said in protest.

It had been more than a year since she and Aidan had played house. In truth, their relationship dissolved long before their divorce, each more interested in their careers than in each other.

Spence was different, Erin told herself. Not that they had a relationship, but everything about him was larger than life. He was exuberant, vital, virile and always smiling. Around Spence, she felt feminine and desired. He entertained her. He laughed at her jokes, swept her into bear hugs, and ate her cooking with courage.

At night, they snuggled into the hammock and watched the stars. He told her about his work, the artists he admired. Supremely confident in all things, still he was amazed that people paid small fortunes for his paintings.

One morning he asked her to pose for him.

All of a sudden Erin felt shy. As an editor, she had worked hard to not intrude in other people's art. She cleaned, pared, molded but never left her own creative mark. To be a part of Spence's painting would leave a permanent mark, she thought.

"I don't think that's a good idea," she said as she pulled the champagne coverlet up to her chin.

"I do. Stay right here."

He returned with a large canvas, his easel and tackle box of paints. She sat, filled with anxiety. He pushed her back on the bed. "I have to hurry. This is the right light," he added. He arranged her arms behind her head and bent one knee. He placed a pillow under her back, thrusting her bra-clad breasts in the air, arranged her hair the way he wanted and stepped back to survey. She felt like a pin-up girl and said so.

"That's it, exactly. Are you familiar with Alberto Vargas?"

"No. Who's he?"

"He's an artist from the 1930s and '40s. He painted the most beautiful women in the world. You must have seen his 'Betty Grable Moon over Miami' poster."

"Is that all I am to you? A pin-up girl?"

"Well, you've got all these nice curves and such big, soft ...."

"All right, I get it. I'm going on a diet tomorrow."

"Oh, no you don't. This painting is going to take a little longer than that."

"You mean I have to lay here all day, nearly naked while you stare at me?"

"And that's different from other days how?"

* * *

By the end of the week, the canvas was taking shape.

Erin was flattered. "I wish I looked that good!"

Inspired, Spence made several pastel sketches of her in various outfits. He asked her to wear only stockings with garters and an apron in one. Another he sketched with her in her red cocktail dress, lying on the sofa. He had tugged the bodice low, with her nipples barely visible. One hand pulled her skirt up her thigh; her other hand was arranged behind her head. He had her keep one leg on the floor, the other bent and on the sofa. She wore her silver shoes and a pair of red panties lay on the floor.

"This is hot," she said.

"You're telling me," he replied.

"I mean, hot hot."

"I'm almost finished."

Soon he put down his pastel crayon and came over to the couch. Sweat beaded on her upper lip as she held the pose.

"Don't move," he whispered. He knelt beside the sofa and kissed her tenderly. Soon his hungry lips were moving on her neck and fastening on her half-hidden nipples. His hand slid under her skirt, and he began rubbing her. Within moments, she was purring into his ear.

"This is what I wanted you to do the first night I wore this," she confessed.

* * *

It had been two months since she had left D.C. Patricia called for an update.

"Erin? How are you and Spence getting along?"

"Fine. Everything's great."

"I'm calling because I've had a chance to review the outline and chapters you've filed. They're great, but I know you can work faster than this. What's the problem?"

"No problem. Everything's great," she repeated. "Spence has been painting a lot lately."

She neglected to say that she was his subject and that when he wasn't painting, they were either in bed making love or eating. It occurred to Erin that the bulk of her time had been spent on pleasing herself and Spence. She hadn't even had time to read the paperbacks she'd brought along.

"Well, you've got him on a schedule, at least, but the quality is not there on these last two chapters. They are too thin and they're primarily technique. We need more input from the artist's point of view. Do a little psycho analyzing, for God's sake. That was your minor in college, wasn't it?"

"Yes, that's right. Will do. Thanks for calling. Bye."

Erin hung up quickly, hoping that Patricia had been stalled.

Spence, who was painting her toenails for his next pin-up poster, asked, "Who was that?"

"Patricia McDowell. She wanted to know how we're doing on the book. I lied, of course."

He lifted her foot, blew on the red polish and smiled wickedly.

"Spence," she said with a sigh. "This is a bit silly, don't

you think? I'm not your doll baby."

"No, you're my pin-up girl. Believe me, there's a difference."

"Haven't I done everything you've asked?"

"Haven't I done everything you've asked?" he echoed.

"Mostly, but it's time to stop playing around."

"But I like to play with you."

"Spence. You're a grown man, and men don't act this way. Quit tickling my feet."

He grinned lecherously. "I know men don't act this way. They just wish they could."

"We need to buckle down and work," she said frowning. "Maybe this house and all of your toys are too much of a distraction. How would you like to come home with me?"

"You mean D.C.?"

Erin shook her head. No, the last thing she wanted was for Spence and Aidan to meet. Aidan. Hmmm, she thought, she hadn't thought of him in a couple of months.

"No, I mean Pennsylvania. Do you remember I told you about my family's cabin at the lake? It's far from everything. We could focus on the book there."

Spence was doubtful.

"I like it here, though. I've got all these sketches going. I think it's a great series. Don't you enjoy working with me?"

"I do; I love it. But Patricia didn't hire me to wear sexy underwear and pose for you. I appreciate the fact that you like my body, but I have a mind, also."

Spence put down the nail polish brush and stared at her in mock horror. She was reclining on the couch, a white fur cape hanging from a shoulder. Faux diamond pendants dangled from her ears. Her lips were vivid red, her eyes ringed with black fake lashes. She wore a black corset that lifted her large breasts out like torpedoes. The corset ended above her navel. A pair of black, lacy panties completed today's ensemble.

"Baby, how could you ask me to give up all of this?" he asked in anguish.

"I think you're over reacting. I think I look slutty."

"You're wrong. You're a goddess." He kissed her cheek, careful not to smudge her red, glistening lips and whispered against her ear. "I've got to sketch you now, while I can still stand up."

Once again, Erin's resolution to buckle down and finish the project dissolved.

CHAPTER FOURTEEN

Erin texted her sister, saying she would be there soon. She recalled the phone conversation and how she had hedged, explaining only that she was bringing a client to work at the cabin.

After twelve hours on the road, the packed SUV cruised down a long, dusty driveway. It stopped in front of a white clapboard house with dark green shutters. In the distance, Spence spied a red barn bearing a large painted star. Chickens bobbed and weaved in the July heat, separated from the driveway by a wire fence. A couple of barn cats, fat and luxuriant, were perched outside the fence, focused on the jerky movements of the plump hens.

A brown painted fence stretched from the barn and into the woods on the far hill. Cattle dotted the hillside, and in a separate, smaller pasture Spence saw white spots.

"Those are sheep," Erin said with an incline of her head. "I told you I was a farm girl. Come on, my sister and her husband are waiting to meet you."

Erin caught Spence's hand and pulled him towards the house as the front porch opened. A tall woman, a faded version of Erin with a few extra pounds on her hips, stepped out and arms open.

Erin dropped Spence's hand and rushed up the steps, sweeping her sister into a bear hug.

"I'm so glad to see you honey," Mariah said, her cheek pressed against her younger sister's golden hair. She looked beyond Erin's shoulder and into Spence's eyes. Her warm smile and green eyes were welcoming. He saw her lips move against Erin's ear but didn't hear her speak, "Oh my, he's gorgeous. I want your job."

* * *

"Mr. Spence, this is your room for tonight," Mariah said, opening the door. "My husband, Jerry, hasn't had a chance yet to air out the cabin. It's been closed up all winter."

White walls painted many years ago had faded to cream. The queen-size bed bore a handcrafted quilt, washed so often its flowers were pastel. A narrow window reached from the floor to the ceiling.

Erin walked over to the window and slid open the curtains, admiring the view, pastoral and green. "I've always loved this room," she said.

Spence moved behind her, slid his arms around her, enveloping her body. He pushed his chin against the back of her neck, his lips caressing her hair. Erin leaned into his embrace.

Mariah's eyes widened as she watched the couple, already oblivious to her. She backed to the bedroom door and slipped out, closing it behind her. She'd suspected from the moment she saw Erin's face, her "client" was much more than that. Their embrace confirmed it.

She went down the stairs and into the farmhouse kitchen. Warm, cozy and filled with century-old wood cabinetry, the kitchen was Mariah's retreat. Dried herbs and flowers hung upside down from the large wooden beams and a copper kettle kept water warm for her frequent cups of tea. Marsh, the family's dog, snored under the spacious oak dining table.

Jerry came in, stamping the mud onto the wooden grate by the back door. He sat on the nearby parson's bench, bent over and began unlacing the work boots. He pulled them off and reached under the bench for his leather mocs.

"Are they settled in? Did you take them to their rooms?"

Mariah smiled impishly, raised her dreamy eyes from a cup of tea. "Room."

Jerry's eyebrows shot up.

Mariah chuckled. "Well, she's allowed."

"Hey," he said, his hands raised in the air. "I say 'Go for it.' What's he like? Bookworm?"

"Not exactly," Mariah said, arching her eyebrows.

Upstairs, Erin held her breath until her chest hurt and sanity returned. She tried to pull away, but the window blocked her escape to the front and Spence's chest, warm and intoxicating against her bare shoulders, eliminated that route. She stepped to the right, but his arms tightened around her rib cage.

"Where are you going?" he said, his breath soft and moist against her neck. His lips caressed her earlobe and she shivered.

"We agreed we wouldn't do this here," she said.

"Don't worry, She's gone."

"That's not the point. You know ...."

"I can't stop, either," he said, finishing her sentence.

Spence stepped back towards the bed and sat, pulling her onto his lap. Antique metal springs squeaked as he swung both of their legs onto the bed. Erin closed her eyes and sighed, warmth spreading as she pressed close to him. He muffled her lips with his, cutting off a throaty gasp.

"Spence. You're not being fair."

He pushed up on one elbow and caressed her heaving breasts.

"I know. I'm sorry. I said I'd behave, but I don't think I can."

Erin sat and stared out the window.

"What's Mariah going to think? She doesn't know about us, about you, except that you're my job. We're here to work."

Erin frowned. "I can't help the way I react to you. It's a natural response because I'm a healthy female and you're a ... ah ..."

He smiled and waited. "What am I?" he prompted, stroking her hip.

"You're a sexy man and you know it. So quit using it against me. You know I'm vulnerable and when you get me started I can't stop. Right in front of my sister, too!"

"I apologize. How can I make it up to you?" he whispered, his lips against her cheek. Then he grabbed her head and noisily kissed her ear.

She laughed and shoved him off the bed. "A wet Willie. That's all I need," she said, wiping her ear.

Downstairs, in the kitchen, Mariah and Jerry heard the thump. A body hitting the floor? The walls of the old farmhouse were too thick to eavesdrop, but they recognized Erin's giggle. They smiled at each other.

"Hey, as long as she likes him, it's okay with me," Jerry said.

"I know. It's her life. But this situation with Aidan ... they still live together."

"They live in the same apartment. It's not the same thing," Jerry said.

"Yes, but it's still complicated."

"Like I said, as long as she likes him and he likes her." Jerry looked up at the ceiling. "It's their business. I don't like to get involved in other people's business."

"You said that already. But she's not 'other people.' She's my sister!"

"And she's an adult. She's taken care of herself for the past ten years; she can take care of herself now. No meddling. Leave them alone," he warned.

Mariah rolled her eyes at her husband.

"I'm not a meddler. But I'm not going to let some playboy artist use my little sister."

"I don't think he's using her."

"How do you know?"

"Knowing your sister, I'm sure she's got him wrapped around her little finger."

Mariah chuckled at her husband's opinion, and hoped he was right.

* * *

An hour later, Erin and Spence rounded the corner of the barn. Ducks and chickens waddled about the yard, scratching and pecking the ground. Marsh, the Australian Shepherd dog, walked behind them, poking Erin's legs with his nose.

"It's his job," Erin said at Spence's quizzical expression. "He thinks I'm one of the sheep and he's trying to tell me where to go. He's not just a sheepdog, he's also a good babysitter. He always kept Mariah's kids in the yard and out of trouble."

"How many children do they have?"

"They have three. Two are grown up, well nearly grown up, and one lives at home. Mariah's a bit older than I am, and she's been married for more than twenty years. Their oldest is Tom. He's nineteen and at college. Samantha, their second, is seventeen and she's a camp counselor during the summer. She's been working at the camp across the lake for three years. When she goes to college she'll probably study sports recreation. She's the tomboy. Then there's Benjamin. He's twelve. He's here somewhere. I guess he has a lot of chores to do during the summer and when he's finished, he jets out. I know I did."

"You grew up on this farm?"

"Yes, it's been in my family for more than a century.

117

When our parents retired, they moved to Florida. It is the law, you know."

"Seems to be."

"Well, I was in college in D.C. and I wasn't interested in the farm, so I sold my half to Mariah and Jerry. That's how I could afford to go to such an expensive university. I had enough left over to stay in D.C. and establish myself as a freelance writer. Eventually, I became an editor with steady jobs."

"Do you like it?"

"Yes indeed. I love editing. I'm a fair writer, but I'm afraid I'm not the creative type. I admire creativity in others and wish I had their talent, but I've become accustomed to the fact that I'm a left-brainer–logical and analytical. You're a right-brain thinker. You're intuitive and artistic."

"Does that mean you're smarter than me?"

"No! I think you're wonderful." She blushed. "I mean, I think your work is wonderful."

Spence smiled at her embarrassment and said nothing.

"Don't torment me."

"Me? I'm innocent. You're the one who's doing all the talking."

"Right, I'll shut up. It's only getting me in trouble."

Spence captured her hand and squeezed it gently. "I like listening to you."

Erin stumbled and Marsh, ever faithful, bumped her behind her knee. Move along. "Okay," she said, laughing. She brushed the dog's soft, furry ears. "I'm going."

They walked, hand-in-hand, to the top of the hill and stopped. Sunlight sparkled off of Breakthrough Lake and, in the distance, small boats sporting white sails dotted the far shore.

"That's the camp where Samantha is. I worked there a couple of years," Erin said. She tugged at his hand, "Come on."

They walked down the hill towards a small, rustic

cabin. Erin stepped onto the porch.

"This is our cabin. Daddy and Mom always brought us here on the weekends during the summer. It was like taking a vacation from the farm, although Daddy could still walk home and take care of the animals. This is where Mariah taught me how to swim and how to sail."

"What did your parents do here?"

"Oh, they relaxed. They fished. Mom read a lot. She never went anywhere without a book."

"What did your Dad like to do?"

"Well, he had to go home every day to feed the livestock, so that took a few hours. He loved to nap in his hammock. He also cooked. Mom would catch fish all day, then he would fry it. He makes the best hush puppies I've ever tasted."

"Sounds like a nice life."

"It was. I had a good childhood and a great family. No hidden demons."

"You're lucky."

"I know. I don't take it for granted. I wish everyone could have had the same kind of childhood. At night Mariah and I would go sneak out on the roof and watch the stars. They're so bright and so close here. Wait until you see them."

"I'm looking forward to it."

* * *

Back at the farmhouse, the kitchen screen door slammed shut.

"Ben! Don't let the door slam," Mariah yelled at her youngest son. "And wipe your feet."

Ben Chappell enjoyed being the only teen at home. Well, almost a teenager. With Sammy at camp, he had exclusive rights to the Xbox. Sure, he had extra chores to do, but he enjoyed his summer of freedom.

"Ben, come here," Mariah called to her youngest, who

had already sat in front of the television and was turning on his video game. Sighing, he tossed the game controls aside and struggled to his feet. "I'm coming."

"What?" He slouched into a chair at the kitchen table. Mariah gave him the "evil eye," her right eyebrow shooting up and her lips a grim line.

"Okay, stop," Ben said, crossing his fingers at his mother and sitting straight in the chair. "Yes, Mother dearest?"

"Your Aunt Erin is here and she's brought a friend. I want you to be on your best behavior. She's working on a book and they need a quiet place. They're going to be using the cabin at the lake while they're here, so you stay out of there. You understand?"

"Sure. I'm not going to bother them. I don't care what they do."

"Make sure you stay out of their way. They're staying here tonight so be polite at the table. Keep your clothes off the bathroom floor, and don't leave the television on too loud or too late."

Great, Ben thought, a perfectly good summer without Sammy and Tom and now Aunt Erin had to ruin it. "I'm not eating dinner here tonight," he said. "Remember? Me and Tommy are going to Peachy's Arcade and then having pizza."

"Tommy and I," Mariah corrected. "And another thing–I think they like each other."

"So?"

"Okay, more than like. I think he's her boyfriend, too."

"What about Aidan?"

"They've been divorced for more than a year."

"Yeah, but don't they still live together?"

"Yes. Not like that, though. Wait a minute...how old are you? What do you know about people living together?"

"Mom, give me a break. I'm not an idiot. Can I go now?"

"Do what I say. You're not too old for a whipping."

"Mom."

"There's always a first time. Now go. Leave me alone. And leave them alone."

Ben retreated to the darkened living room to his new Halo game and Xbox, Erin and her new "boyfriend" already forgotten.

CHAPTER FIFTEEN

While Spence walked the lakeshore, Erin opened the cabin windows letting in the fresh air. She peeked in all of the cabinets, checking out the food situation. She found some staples, such as flour and sugar, in plastic containers, and several bottles of wine. Over the sink, colorful fiesta ware plates and bowls lined the wall. The cabin's furnishings were so old they were back in style.

"Wow. This is Retro," Erin said aloud.

The counter sported a chrome toaster from the 1950s, a blender (Mom's penchant for Margaritas), and a waffle iron. All were old and heavy.

The aqua refrigerator hummed, still running smoothly. Inside was an open box of baking soda. Going to need some supplies, she thought.

The cabin's floor plan was simple. It had one bedroom, one bathroom, and a great room that served as a kitchen, dining and living room. When they were young, Mariah and Erin had slept on cots on the screened porch. All of the furniture was the same as she remembered except for the new sleep sofa. Mariah and Jerry had purchased it for Tom when, as he grew older, he refused to spend summer nights on the porch with Sammy and Ben.

"So is it livable?" Spence asked, stepping through the open door.

"Sure. Mariah's family uses it during the summer, so everything works. This is the first time it's been opened this year, so it's a bit musty."

"What's next?"

"I've got to go to the store and get some supplies. I guess I should make a shopping list. We should get a coffee pot, too."

She pulled a reporter's notebook from her back pocket and slid an ink pen out of its wire coils. She sat on the sofa and patted the cushion next to her.

"Here, sit down. Tell me what you want."

Spence didn't hesitate. He dived onto the couch and laid his head on her lap, curling an arm around her neck.

"Baby, you know what I want."

"No, silly," Erin said bending closer to his face. She closed her eyes anticipating the touch of his lips. "I mean from the store," she whispered.

"I know what you mean. Kiss me."

"One kiss. Then help me make a list," Erin conceded.

"One kiss it is," Spence said. His right arm pinned against the sofa, he grabbed a handful of her soft hair and pulled her head back, baring her creamy throat. With his left hand, he began unbuttoning her shirt.

"Hey, I said one kiss."

"Give me a minute. I'm getting there."

Erin turned her head and kissed his wrist, her lips against his pulse. She closed her eyes as he unclasped her bra (darn those front enclosures! Okay, maybe not) and stroked her breasts.

"Is it a kiss if it's here?" Spence asked.

"Mmmmmmmaybe."

He nuzzled the cleft between her ribs and then traced a path back to her breast, his tongue hot and wet.

"Make up your mind. Quick."

"Umm, no."

"No what? No, it's not kiss, or no, you won't make up your mind?" he murmured.

"No, it's not a kiss."

Erin grabbed his ears and pulled his mouth onto her breast. She could feel the heat building between her legs. "Better stop."

"You said one kiss. I haven't kissed you yet."

Erin tried to capture his lips, but he turned his head.

"You're so smart," she whispered into his ear, then biting it in spite. Spence retaliated.

"Ow! Meanie."

Spence murmured against her skin, "Let me make it better."

Her shirt swung open. What a dilemma, she thought. Then, she stopped thinking. "You're good."

"What can I say? You bring out the best in me."

"Kiss me. Please."

* * *

That evening, Mariah watched as her sister and the artist strolled through the pasture towards the house. The sunset bathed them in glorious shades of blue, mauve, and orange.

They were holding hands and laughing as they made their way through thigh-high wildflowers. Spence stopped, picked a purple coneflower and tucked it in Erin's hair.

"Work, my ass," Mariah said to Marsh. "Wish I had a job like him."

The dog's tail thumped twice against the wood floor. He was used to Mariah talking aloud. It was a comforting sound and often meant she would toss him a treat. Jerry, who had caught his wife's words as he passed the hallway, followed her gaze out the window.

He smiled, and then came up behind Mariah. He slipped his arms around her waist and nuzzled her neck.

Sex certainly is infectious, she thought, and she turned in his arms and kissed him.

"You want your dinner?" she asked.

"What's behind Door Number Two?"

She smiled at her husband. Taking his strong, calloused hand in hers, she led him out of the kitchen.

* * *

After dinner, Erin opened the bedroom door, flicked on the light switch and stood aside.

"This is your room. I'll be in Sammy's room. It used to be mine, and since she's at camp I'll be using it again."

Mournfully, Spence glanced at the bed, then at Erin. Then back to the bed.

"Baby, aren't you sleeping with me?"

"Calm down, tiger. Today was an exception. You're back on rations. We've got work to do."

"I'll go on strike."

"You can't do that. This isn't a democracy. You've signed a contract and already spent your deposit. We are going to turn out ten pages a day, regardless. We came here to clear our heads and quit acting like rabbits."

Spence sat on the bed, dejected. "I can't believe you're cutting me off."

"It's a distraction and it's impeding your progress," Erin said.

Spence, pretending to be hurt, looked away.

"Now stop that. The bathroom is down the hall, first door on the right. If you need anything, my room is next to it."

"Where do your sister and her husband sleep?"

They have the north wing. They've removed several walls and created a master bedroom and bath. It's luxurious. Do you want to see it?"

"No thanks. I don't intrude in other people's private space."

"You intrude in mine whenever you want."

"Your space is mine."

He pulled her between his knees, wrapping his arms around her hips.

She melted against him as he caressed her, sliding his fingers under her shirt and up her back. She leaned forward and pulled his head to her breasts. He nuzzled her through the fabric, grabbing her shirt in his teeth and pulling a button open.

"Ah, ah, ah," Erin said, pulling away. "It's bedtime and you need your rest. We have to get up early tomorrow and get to work. Remember, Patricia's breathing down my neck to get this project done."

"I just want one ..."

"Sorry. No can do," she said as she walked to the door. "Goodnight, Spence."

In her old bedroom, Erin sat on a chaise and kicked off her flip-flops. She leaned against the wall and sighed. Oh, that gorgeous man, she thought. It wasn't fair. He was too handsome, too funny and smart. And, too good in bed, she added. She closed her eyes and hugged herself, smiling.

After a few moments of self-satisfaction, Erin opened her eyes and admired the room. The walls had long been stripped of the flowered wallpaper of her youth and replaced with blue paint. Posters of sports figures plastered the walls. Spectacular photographs of people snowboarding, skateboarding, surfing, kicking soccer balls and shooting baskets dominated, although there were some hunky singers and actors in the mix.

A portrait sat on the dresser. Erin picked it up and admired the Chappell family. Mariah and Jerry flanked by their children, Marsh the dog and Sammy's cat, Mr. Jinks. They were so happy. Erin ached with sweetness of the scene and her own desire for a family like Mariah's.

A light rap at the door startled her out of her reverie.

"Go away, Spence."

"It's not Spence," Mariah whispered.

"Oops. Sorry." Erin opened the door.

Mariah noted the framed photograph in Erin's hand.

"This is beautiful," Erin said, placing it back on the dresser. "You're so lucky."

"Thank you. It's hard sometimes, but it's always been and always will be the best part of my life."

Erin put her arms around her sister and leaned her head against the taller woman's shoulder. Mariah patted her arm.

"I wanted to make sure you had everything you need. I'm sorry I assumed you two would be sharing a room. I, uh, thought that you, uh ..."

Erin giggled. "I know. It's hard to explain. I'm not sure I even know what's happening. I need my own space, though."

Mariah, spotting an opening, sat on the chaise. She smiled with encouragement.

Embarrassed, Erin sat on the bed and studied her nails. "Like I said, it's hard to explain. I got a call from one of my regular publishers. They have a contract with an artist who needed help finishing a book. He gets distracted easily and wasn't meeting his deadlines. The project is important to them."

Mariah smiled again.

"The arrangement was straightforward. Patricia hired me to be a live-in, editorial nanny, of sorts. That means I keep him on target, help him with his outlines, take dictation, clean up his rough drafts, and make him stick to a word count."

Mariah nodded again, patiently waiting for the juicy bits.

"It was fine, at first. I left Aidan in charge of the apartment. He hasn't talked to me since the first day of the assignment. You know, he's still looking for a place, so I've let him use the second bedroom for a while. It's hard to find nice apartments at a reasonable price in D.C. I leased a car and drove out to the Outer Banks, to an island called Ocracoke. It's spectacular. Birds everywhere." Erin's face became dreamy as she described the house.

"It's remarkable. It's like living inside a glass box, it has so many windows. The walls are white, a gallery for Spence's paintings. Oh, Mariah. Wait 'til you see his paintings. They're so beautiful. His colors are so rich, so saturated and so ... um ... so sexy. His paintings are among the most exciting work on the contemporary art market. Universities offer classes that study his technique. That's why the publisher wants the book."

Mariah leaned back and crossed her arms. "You know enough about art to help him write this book?"

"No, but I don't have to. Like I said, my job is to keep him on target, persuade him to talk about his art and about his life. That's the hard part. He's so reserved. People think he's standoffish, but he's incredibly shy."

Mariah chuckled. "Shy, eh? He doesn't look shy to me."

Erin blushed and averted her eyes. "You've got to remember, we've been working together for a couple of months, so we know each other better. He's comfortable with me. I know; there's something between us. It's not ethical, but I can't keep my hands off of him."

Mariah arched an eyebrow at Erin's confession.

"I can handle it," Erin said, but she wondered if that were true. "I don't want a relationship. Not that he wants one, either. It's a physical thing. I know that. Once the job is over, that's it. I'm back in D.C."

Mariah wasn't convinced. "You say this is just a fling?"

"Yes. No. I'm not sure what it is. God, he's so handsome and sweet. From the beginning he's been so kind to me. I feel guilty. I was hired to work with a headstrong artist and instead I've been on a tropical vacation with sexiest man I've ever met."

Erin ducked her head in shame. Mariah waited.

"He's a dedicated artist and it's amazing to watch him paint. I'm lucky, I guess. He trusts me."

"You think he trusts you?"

"Oh yes. I know he does."

Erin had always been confident as a child, but Mariah could tell from her bravado that she wasn't as sure of herself in this situation.

"Well, call me crazy but I don't think you're walking away from this as easily as you say."

"What are you saying? That I'm in love with him?"

Mariah didn't miss Erin's nervous laugh. "Maybe. Just be careful. You've got a good life in Washington. I'm worried that you'll get too involved and be hurt."

"Oh, don't worry about me. I learned my lesson with Aidan."

Mariah stood and gave her sister a warm, comforting hug. "Okay. Go to bed, sis. We don't give wakeup calls around here. The roosters take care of that."

"Goodnight."

Erin slept restlessly that night, kicking the covers off and then pulling them back on. She hugged one of the pillows and told herself, "I'm asleep." It didn't work. By two o'clock, she gave up and, grabbing one of her pillows, tiptoed down the hall to Spence's room. She turned the doorknob and peeked in.

Moonlight flooded the room and she could hear Spence's gentle breathing. She reached out and touched his bare chest.

"Spence?"

"What? Is everything okay?"

"I miss you."

Spence slid over in the bed and swept the covers to the side. Erin curled against his chest, hugging her pillow. He dropped the blanket and tucked it around her.

"Better?"

"Oh yes."

"Goodnight, sweetheart."

It may have been dawn, but if it was, only the rooster

could tell. Spence jerked awake at the eerie screech.

"What the heck is that?"

"It's the rooster," Erin murmured sleepily. She rolled over, facing Spence and put her extra pillow over their heads. "This will help."

But it didn't. Spence could feel her breath, silky on his face. He became all too aware of her leg between his. Her hand rested against his chest, rubbing it in her sleep. He couldn't see. The pillow created a feeling of sensory deprivation, heightening his other senses. He kissed Erin's nose and she grunted softly, moved closer. He touched her breast. Flannel? Was this some kind of nightgown? Like a blind man, he explored with his fingers, moving over lace, buttons and what felt like small knots. Flowers? The nightgown buttoned down the front to her knees.

Erin woke to the sensation of Spence's hands over her breasts. He kissed each one.

"Good morning, sweetheart."

"Spence? I was dreaming about you."

"Yes?" he asked, taking advantage of her distraction. His fingers sought warmth between her thighs and he caressed her.

"Oh, what a nice way to wake up," Erin said, sighing. "I like it when you do that."

Her skin tingled at his touch. This is so right, she thought. Could this be love? How could it not be? The idea drugged Erin. Each kiss, stroke of his finger, soft bite and lick became a heightened sensation. He feels it too, she thought, as their kiss slowed and deepened. His hands stilled and for an eternity they connected only through their lips. Their breathing synchronized. She could feel his pulse in his tongue, felt as it picked up.

Ah yes.

Spence growled softly and swung his leg over Erin. He pinned her hands behind her head, burying them in the soft pillow. Then, he entered and they fused. He paused at Erin's gasp but then she bucked against the savage sensation and begged for more. She marveled at the blending of his strength and her softness.

Inevitably, he sank into her arms and she kissed his cheeks, his ears and neck, cooing. Their heartbeats slowed and they lay on the bed watching the sun rise. Erin had so much to say, but couldn't open her mouth. Her lips felt dry and bruised, her throat parched. Her body ached, yet she cherished each throb. Spence pulled the blanket over them and tucked her against his chest. She yawned, closed her eyes and fell back asleep.

CHAPTER SIXTEEN

That morning, the family gathered in the farmhouse kitchen. The windows were open to the July breeze and the sounds of livestock: chickens clucking, cows mooing and Marsh, the sheepdog, barking at an errant sheep.

"I love cooking with this old, black frying pan," Jerry said.

The official cook of all egg dishes, he whisked a dozen fresh eggs into a yellow froth. "Cheesy, scrambled eggs are my specialty," he said, winking at Erin.

"Spence, why don't you get the orange juice out of the 'fridge and pour everyone a round?" Mariah asked as she put a platter of bacon on the table.

Erin rose to help but Spence put a staying hand on her shoulder. "I can handle this. You keep buttering the biscuits."

In Spence's honor, Mariah had made a Southern-style, country breakfast, which included grits.

"Can't get this kind of service at those Waffle Houses in the South," she joked.

"You're right about that, ma'am," Spence said, his North Carolina drawl more prominent this morning.

Ben, who hadn't had a chance to meet Spence the day before, looked with interest at their guest.

"You're a Confederate?" he asked.

"A Southerner," Spence explained. "Confederates went out of style after the Civil War. Now we're plain old Americans, just like ya'll."

Ben, already forgetting Mariah's warning, began his favorite game of Twenty Questions.

"Where do you live? The ocean? What kind of boat do you have? Wow; how fast have you gone? Yeah, I can sail, but I'd prefer your speedboat. What do you do? What kind of art? Oh, like that dude Van Gogh? You make much money? You rich? That's cool. You play sports? Any good? Did you play pro ball? Really? Get outta here. No way. How long? What happened? That sucks. You married? No? Got any kids? Well, how am I supposed to know, Mom? People have kids nowadays without being married. All right, I will. Sorry Mr. Spence. Sorry Aunt Erin."

Erin, breathless from watching the Ben-Spence marathon, couldn't believe that a twelve-year-old kid could get more out of Spence in three minutes than she had in two months.

"You played baseball?"

"When I was younger. That was a long time ago,"

He reached under the table and squeezed her hand, then held it in his lap. Mariah, who noticed the gesture from her vantage point at the stove, ignored it. Sure, she can handle him, Mariah thought.

"We're going to the store after breakfast. You need anything?" Erin asked.

"I thought you took care of that yesterday. I'm sorry, was the cabin that much of a mess that it took you all afternoon to get it ready?" Mariah replied.

Erin opened her mouth, then abruptly closed it when she recalled how she spent her afternoon. "No; it was fine. We did a little exploring."

"That's right. We were exploring." Spence echoed.

Ben piped in, "Hey, I know some good places. Let me know next time you guys go exploring and I'll come with you."

Spence grinned and said, "Sure will, Ben. Thanks."

Mariah gave Ben her evil eye. "What did I tell you yesterday? You go about your business and you leave them alone. They're working."

Jerry broke into the fray, bearing a bowl of steaming eggs. "Ah, perfect. Now, dig in everybody. Even bookworms need a good breakfast to start the day."

Mariah turned her evil eye on her husband.

* * *

On the way to town, Erin chatted about Eaton, so named for a prominent pioneer. About 2,000 inhabitants were scattered throughout the mountainsides, most on farms settled in the late 1700s and early 1800s, with another 8,000 in town. The jewel of the region was Breakthrough Lake, spring fed and crystal clear.

Surrounded by verdant forests of white pine, cypress and hemlock, the lake had become a resort in the early 1900s. Wealthy families yearning to escape the city during the summer would flock to the lakeshore. Some built extravagant lodges; others built small one-room cabins like the Andersen's. Their bedroom and bathroom had been an addition built in the 1950s when the newly married couple was expecting their first child.

Breakthrough Lodge had become a popular retreat. Through the years it evolved into a youth camp. Teens in the area loved it because it meant summer jobs and short romances with city girls and boys.

When Erin worked at Breakthrough Lodge, she also had a summer romance. It lasted for two years. She even selected the same college as her boyfriend.

"Eventually," she said, "we got married."

"What? You're married?" Spence was incredulous.

"No. Not anymore. We've been divorced for a year."

"When were you going to tell me?"

Erin didn't answer. She hadn't thought about telling him about Aidan because, well, because when they first met it wasn't his business. Theirs was a working relationship and he didn't need to know about her personal life. Then, when things changed, and they changed so quickly, she didn't even think about Aidan. Spence dominated her thoughts as easily as he dominated her body.

She glanced at Spence. He was staring out the passenger window, frowning. She had never seen him angry.

Ten interminable minutes later Erin pulled into the half-empty lot of Peachy's, the area's grocery store. Once a mom-and-pop operation, it had been in business since 1842. It had evolved from a feed store into a general store, and now served as the area's grocery/video/gas station/beauty salon/pet store. Each generation of the Peachy family had added on to the business, expanding it as their various interests and talents emerged.

Cindy Peachy ran the gas station, smiling at customers while she checked their oil and washed their windows. She took pride in offering good, old-fashioned service.

"Well, hey girl. Long time no see," she called out when Erin exited the SUV. Cindy's eyes widened when she saw Spence. She closed her yap; she'd ask Mariah about her sister's new man later, she thought.

Erin waved and smiled, but her heart wasn't in it. "Hi Cindy."

She pulled a shopping cart from the corral and headed for the store. Spence followed in silence.

To the uninitiated eye, Peachy's was monstrous. Through the years and as the business diverged, haphazard additions were slapped together. The people of Eaton understood this. Newcomers, however, weren't impressed.

"This place is hideous," Spence said, adding. "Well, most of it."

Erin lifted her chin. "I think the place is great," she said defensively.

She followed his gaze and noted a new business in the complex–an open-air coffee house. Wrought iron draped with realistic grapevines camouflaged the ceiling. Pretty wrought iron tables were arranged in groupings on the new terra cotta-tiled floor. Water gurgled from the large fountain. She sniffed in appreciation at the aroma of exotic coffee blends and fresh cooked pastries.

"That's nice! Another Peachy has come home," she said.

As she and Spence surveyed the cafe a movement from one corner caught her eye. Behind the counter, a young woman operated an espresso machine.

"That's Shelia Peachy," Erin said. "She must have opened this café after culinary school. Have I been gone that long?"

The sound of metal scraping tile caught her attention and she turned to see Katrina Hall, a beautiful prissy-pot she knew from high school, stand abruptly from one of the iron chairs. She knocked over a cup of coffee and it poured onto the tabletop and began to drip right into a designer handbag.

Erin smirked as the woman swore aloud and grabbed napkins, dabbing at the spill. The guy with her, a hunk in jeans and a flannel shirt, was unperturbed. Erin didn't recognize him and wondered if he was new in town. She snickered at Katrina's dilemma and when Spence eyed her quizzically, Erin said, "She was a stuck-up snot when I knew her in school. Nice to see karma in action."

Spence watched the interplay between the enraged beauty queen and her companion and noticed that despite her apparent hostility at the guy, she sat. He couldn't figure out whether she liked him or not. He sighed knowing that women would always be a mystery to him.

As they moved through the entrance, Billy Peachy glanced up from his station in the hair salon. "Erin," he called. "Welcome home. Give me a call and I'll squeeze you in."

Spence looked at the empty salon, then at the effeminate young man teasing the hair of the sole customer, an elderly woman.

"Squeeze you in?" he muttered.

"Thanks Billy. I'll call you," Erin promised.

Spence paused at a sign calling for investors. "Somebody's got big plans for the place," he said.

Erin read the sign and admired architect Jack Frey's drawing of the new and improved Peachy's. Jack's mother was a Peachy and she still operated the fitness center that also offered video and DVD rentals. "Wow! Eaton will finally get a shopping mall!"

Spence eyed the cacophony of storefronts, each opened individually and without much regard for the design or location of its neighbor. One window featured wrestling puppies under the shop name, "Mazie's Pet Store." Around the corner was a chiropractor. Someone had plunked a jewelry kiosk in the walkway next to the arcade.

"Is there anything this place doesn't have?" Spence asked.

"It's got a boutique and a gun shop, but it could use a Gap. Or Peachy's version of the Gap," Erin suggested. "Now's the time to get in on the action. Want to invest some of those millions?"

A grim Spence smiled but said nothing.

Mac Peachy, Billy's grandfather, was stocking the cereal aisle as they rounded the corner and entered the grocery store.

"Erin, nice to see you," he said. "Good day, sir. Welcome to Eaton and to Peachy's."

Spence dipped his head to the courtly old gentleman. He noted the box of bran flakes in Mac's hand. "Excuse me, do you carry Captain Crunch?"

"Ah, a sweet tooth. All filling and no fiber but yes, we carry it. Down aisle seven on the right."

Erin smiled at Mac and maneuvered the cart down the aisle. Spence dropped two boxes of cereal in the basket. Erin picked up a box of shredded wheat.

"I prefer substance," she said.

Silent and moody, they worked their way through each aisle, dropping items helter skelter into the basket.

"Don't they sell beer or wine here?" Spence asked.

"You have to go to a package store for that. Alcohol is only sold in state stores."

"That's ridiculous. What if I want a glass of wine my meal?"

Erin sighed. "I have wine at the cabin."

They checked out silently; Erin insisted on paying for the food. At the SUV, Spence loaded the grocery bags into the back compartment. Slamming the hatch shut, he moved to the driver's side.

"Give me the keys," he demanded.

"You don't know where you're going," Erin argued.

"I'll figure it out. There's only one road."

Erin stared at his chin then flipped him the keys. He caught them high in the air. Then, taking her elbow he escorted her to the passenger side. He opened the door and waited for her to slide in before closing it quietly.

Erin wanted to shriek. Spence climbed in and as he was placing the key into the ignition, Erin put her hand on his arm.

"Please don't do this."

"Do what?"

"Don't be angry. No silent treatment. If you have anything to say, then say it. I said I was sorry. I didn't see how it could matter."

"You've been living with me for weeks and you didn't think it could matter that you're married?"

"We're not 'living together' and I'm not married!"

"Why didn't you tell me?"

"Because he doesn't matter."

"How could he not?"

"Spence, you've been with many beautiful women. I know; I've seen the magazines." She slid next to him and put her arms around his neck, pressing her cheek to his. "Do you think about them when you're with me?"

His arms tightened around her and he kissed her, punishing her with his angry mouth. Despite the pain, Erin welcomed his touch, her lips pliant against his. He shoved her away, turned to the steering wheel and started the engine. The truck tires spun as he pulled out of the parking lot and headed towards the Chappell farm.

He was going too fast and he knew it, blowing past the 55 speed limit sign. Uncomfortable, Erin squirmed as the red speedometer needle rose to 70. As she started to speak and caution him to slow down, they both heard a "whrrppp" and saw red flashing lights in their side mirrors.

A frown creased Spence's face as he moved his foot from the gas pedal and braked. He put on a turn signal and looked ahead for a turn-off. With no shoulder on the country road, he waited for a driveway and then pulled in. The old farmhouse it served was set a quarter mile off the road so he didn't think they would mind.

"Great," Erin muttered. "This is all we need."

Soon, a tall, dark-haired man, his eyes shuttered with dark sunglasses and a police-issue Stetson on his head, appeared at the driver's side door of the SUV. Spence rolled down the window and had his wallet in his lap, searching for his license.

"Hi Boone! How you doing?" Erin flashed a dazzling smile at the man.

Spence glanced at Erin then back at the police officer, and watched her turn on the charm.

"Didn't I hear that you're the sheriff now? That's awesome. How's your mom? Your daddy still preaching at the Baptist church?"

Sheriff Alec Boone smiled. "Hello Erin. It's good to

see you again." He turned back to Spence and said, "License and registration please."

Spence handed him his North Carolina license and looked to Erin for the paperwork. She opened the glove box and pulled out the contract. "It's not our car. It's a lease. Spence and I just arrived in town and he's not used to the roads here yet," she said, explaining.

"It's fine," Spence growled at Erin. To Boone he said, "It's okay. I know I was speeding. Write the ticket and we'll be on our way."

Erin chewed her lip and peered out the passenger window.

Boone read the license and the car lease info. He handed them to Spence and tipped his hat back. He recognized tension and figured the man was clenching his jaw because of the woman next to him, not concern for a speeding ticket. He'd been repressing a lot of his own frustration lately.

"No ticket, just a warning. Keep your eye open for deer, also. They can do a lot of damage, even to a large vehicle like this." Boone ducked a little lower and smiled at Erin. "Erin, have a nice day. Yes, daddy's still preaching and mama is fine. I'll tell her you said, 'Hello.'"

Spence watched his side mirror as the tall man sauntered back to his police car. When the door closed and the flashing lights turned off, he turned towards Erin.

"Is your seatbelt fastened?" he asked. With a nod, he turned on his blinker and backed out of the driveway and onto the highway. It was a quiet ride the rest of the way to the cabin. It was, after all, only one road and he did recall the way.

Spence helped unload the grocery bags and then headed out the door. "I'm going for a walk."

Erin watched as he strode the path to the shore. A tear slid down the side of her nose. She sniffed, then turned to the kitchen cabinets and began putting away the food. She decided to grill steaks, and pulled a bottle of merlot from the wine rack. She popped the cork and filled two glasses with the deep red wine.

With her left hand clutching her wine glass and a bag of charcoal in the other, she walked outside. Setting her glass on the picnic table, she ripped the bag open and spilled the contents into the grill. She squirted lighter fluid on the briquettes and inhaled as she lit them, cravenly enjoying the dizzy rush from the fumes. Soon the charcoal glowed red beneath a layer of white ash. She hoped Spence would smell the steaks and realize his would be well done. Too well done.

Fine, she thought, tipping her third glass of wine at the clock, let him stay outside, in the woods. Probably lost. She took another deep gulp. Hope he's out there all night. Hope he's freezing.

She piled a salad of mixed greens, walnuts and strawberries on the bright blue fiesta ware plates. The table, heavy with its Formica top and chrome legs, was another "Retro" treasure. She broke a loaf of French bread in half, and then into smaller chunks, arranging them in a basket lined with a red-checked napkin. A generous dollop of butter in a small, avocado-green bowl completed the scene.

Steaks, salad, bread, wine. All the ingredients were there except for Spence. Where was he? Erin tipped the bottle of wine, filling her glass again. Darn, now the bottle's empty. No matter; she picked up Spence's glass and sipped his. Serves him right. I'll eat his steak, too.

Erin curled on the sofa and waited, the pink vintage radio playing Golden Oldies.

Mom, Dad? Where are you? How did I make such a mess? Erin emptied the wine glass and, leaning back, closed her eyes.

It was much later when Spence mounted the cabin steps and opened the screen door. A soft light glowed in one corner of the room. The kitchen table had been set for two, a romantic dinner. An empty bottle of wine sat on the counter, a goblet in the sink.

Erin, asleep on the couch, had curled into a ball still clutching the other goblet. Her light hair fanned her cheek. Spence took the glass out of her relaxed fingers and knelt on the floor beside the sofa. He stroked her cheek and whispered her name.

"Spence?" She roused slowly, groggy still from drinking too much wine.

"You partying without me?"

"I waited long as I could. I'm sorry." She snuggled against his hand and kissed his knuckles. "Don't leave me, Spence."

"I'm not, baby. I'm here."

"I'm sorry. I didn't mean to tell you. I mean, I didn't want you to find out... I don't know what I'm saying. Stop me," she said, drowsily stroking his cheek.

He bent to her lips, tasting the wine and breathing in the heady aroma of spirits and her clean, female scent. "Woman, you make me crazy."

Erin put her arms around his neck. "Shhh. Kiss me."

Dinner forgotten, Spence did as he was told.

CHAPTER SEVENTEEN

"**O**kay, its Day Three in Pennsylvania and we really have to get some work done," Erin said. She flipped open her laptop and plugged it into the nearest outlet. Booting her computer, she clicked on the word processing icon. She typed a heading then waited for Spence.

He lolled on the sofa bed, his hair wet from their late morning swim. They spent the night at the cabin, enjoying make-up sex, then again in the lake that morning.

"We've only got a bare-bones outline and a few raggedy-ass chapters. We have to move on. Patricia is going to fire me if I can't get you motivated."

"Erin, I don't have time to write a book. I'm too busy slaking my editor's lust."

She blushed and tossed a cinnamon bun at his head. He caught it and took a bite.

"Lord, if you would only work as hard on this book as you do making excuses."

"Let's make a deal: You give me a massage and I'll work steady for one hour." He rolled over, crossed his arms under his chin and winked at her. His hair, tousled with streaks of brown and red, shone like gold in the morning sun. His smile, white teeth against his tanned face, took her breath away. Does he know how beautiful he is, she wondered. Dazzled, she stood and walked over to the sofa bed. She stumbled over the covers, kicked off the night before.

"Ooof," she gasped as she fell against the arm of the sofa.

"Easy, easy," he drawled, stretching out an arm to help her up. "Don't injure yourself. I really need this massage."

She picked up the vial of lotion they had experimented with hours earlier and squirted some into her palm. She rubbed her hands together to warm the cream. Then, straddling his hips, she leaned over and began working her fingers into his muscled upper arms. "I like my men strong."

"Mm hmm," he replied.

She put more lotion in her hands and then, impishly, squirted a zigzag on his back. She kneaded his shoulders and pressed her thumb into a knot.

"Ow. That hurts!"

"It's supposed to. It's a trigger point. I press hard and it releases. That means the muscle relaxes."

"Where'd you learn that?"

"I worked one summer at Peachy's Chiropractic Clinic. Jimmy Peachy's a doctor."

"Chiropractors aren't doctors."

"Of course they are."

"Whatever."

Spence relaxed under Erin's care, and soon he was snoring. She tweaked his nose. "Hey, wake up. You promised to work for an hour."

He sat reluctantly, and started unbuttoning her shirt. "Your turn."

"I don't need a massage."

"Oh yes you do." He unclasped her bra, the straps falling off her shoulders. As she reached for her straps to pull it back on, Spence caught her wrists and tucked both of them behind her back.

"Fine, keep your shirt on," he said as he pushed the sleeves down her arms.

"Let go of me you galoot."

"In a minute," he said, tweaking her nose.

Erin leaned back, watching him mistrustfully. Her hands were pinned behind her and his added weight kept them there. Spence held the tube over her and squeezed. A line of cucumber lotion flowed onto her skin. She sucked her breath at the cold and her belly danced. He drew lines and symbols across her breasts. Dots and dashes marched up her neck and out her collar bones.

"Just like painting," he said. He tossed the tube aside and started rubbing the lotion into her skin, massaging her gently. "There's a lot more to painting than you know. I have to spend hours watching the light as it changes. Just like the hours you spend correcting the commas in somebody's manuscript. It's a work in progress."

"I guess I never thought about it that way. Tell me more."

"Does this count towards that hour?"

"Oh come on, do you think this is work? I'm a captive here. I can't even scratch my nose."

"Here, let me." Spence rubbed greasy fingers on her nose, leaving a glob of lotion in his wake.

"Yeah, thanks. That helps."

It was hard to be flippant, though, with his fingers working magic on her skin, caressing her breasts, tickling her ribs. With his free hand, he fiddled at the button on her shorts and pulled down the short zipper. "Good. These are easy."

He tugged her shorts off her hips and tossed them on the floor. "Pretty," he said, admiring her panties.

"They better be; they're expensive for such a scrap of material."

"It looks like an eye patch. Can I borrow them?"

Erin laughed at the image of Spence, a pair of her fancy

thong panties rakishly covering one eye.

"Whatever wags your tail."

"What does that mean?"

"A happy puppy wags its tail. If it makes you happy, do it."

"Thanks, ma'am. Think I will."

With that, Spence proceeded to kiss and lick Erin's belly and the inside of her thighs. His hand caressed her breasts. Soon she was dragging her hands through his hair, craving his touch. Within minutes she was gasping for air as wave after wave of ecstasy raced through her. She pushed him away and rolled to her side, squeezing her knees together.

"Go away," she said, covering her eyes with her hands.

"Baby, did I hurt you?"

"No, no. I'm so embarrassed. Spence, how am I supposed to work with you when you do this to me? I feel so exposed. You're everywhere. Can't you see how difficult all this is?"

"Sure I do. You turn me inside out and then you want to write about it. How is that not supposed to embarrass me?"

Erin uncovered her eyes. Spence's head was turned away, his jaw clenching. She reached out to stroke his cheek, softening it with her gentle touch.

He turned and buried his face in her neck. Then he scooped her into his lap and rocked her back and forth. She wondered: Who is he comforting?

* * *

"How's it going? You two making any progress?" Mariah asked when Erin returned to the farmhouse at the end of the week to do some laundry.

She grimaced as she packed more clothes into the washing machine. She sprinkled powdered detergent into the cavity, closed the door and turned the knob. Leaning against the machine, she turned back to her sister.

"That's a good question."

"Well?"

Erin flashed a grin at Mariah, and looked away. It was a guilty reaction that Mariah recognized from their childhood.

"I appreciate your hospitality. I know I said it was going to be all work and no play. I meant it, too. That's why I made him come here. I thought that if I had him on my own turf, I could control him. Keep him on task and get some chapters written."

"What's the problem?"

"I don't think I can control him at all."

"Is that so bad?"

Erin snorted and laughed. "Yes, it is actually. I can't even control myself. I can't keep my pants on around him."

Now it was Mariah's turn to laugh. Her sister, always so competent, had lost the upper hand.

"Yikes; you've got a big problem."

"I can handle it."

"I could too, if I weren't a married woman."

Erin laughed and whacked her sister with a dish towel.

"Go jump Jerry's bones. I'll take care of Spence."

"Don't think I haven't been. You're my inspiration."

* * *

Erin and Spence were floating on the lake, a white rope connecting their inner tubes to a cooler of chilled beer. Erin's hand dangled lazily in the water; the other tipped the beer to her lips. Corona with a lime.

"This is heavenly."

Spence squinted one eye, the other covered with a pair of her panties.

"You idiot." She laughed. It felt so nice to be relaxing in the sun, this stunning man beside her, making jokes for her pleasure. "You are such a goof. What if Ben sees you?"

"Arr, matey. I'm sure the lad knows what an eye patch is."

Spence had been on his pirate kick for the past hour, and together they had worked their way through a six pack. She thought of pirates and Tortuga and, for a second, swore she could smell peach juice.

"You know, you could pay me to work for you and we could do this all the time," she quipped.

"Maybe I will."

Erin backpedaled. "I'm kidding."

"Maybe I'm not."

"Do you ever intend to write this book?"

He raised his "eye patch" but didn't answer.

"I'm just asking. Because ethically, if you're not, I have to let the publisher know. I have a responsibility. I've never missed a deadline."

"Never?"

"Never."

"Even in high school? On your student newspaper?"

"How did you know I worked on the newspaper?"

"Darlin', I know you. You were probably an editor then, too."

Erin stuck out her bottom lip. "Smarty pants." She kicked the water, splashing him in the face.

* * *

By the end of their second week in Pennsylvania, Erin and Spence had given up any pretense of working. They stayed at the cabin, rising later each morning, eating in bed, lounging in the hammock and swimming in the lake. After dinner they sat around, toothpicks in their mouths, and played Texas Hold 'Em. Sometimes they played strip poker, but only after they put on several layers of clothing. They didn't want to lose too quickly.

Time meant little; the days ticked off like seconds on a

clock. One evening, they were sitting around the Formica dining table. Erin wore three shirts and a pair of shorts over a pair of pants. Beneath that, she wore her bathing suit. Spence was down to a pair of boxers and a T-shirt. He still had his socks and shoes, his eyepatch, and a faded ball cap pulled low to hide his poker face.

Jerry knocked on the screen door. "You guys decent?" he called.

Startled, their eyes met. They never had visitors to the cabin. Sometimes they imagined they were alone in the world; the only other signs of life were miniature people sailing miniature boats across the lake.

Spence opened the door. Jerry looked at him, then at Erin.

"You guys cold out here? There's a radiant heater in the attic."

"No. Not at all. We're playing strip poker," Erin said.

Jerry nodded as if he understood. "Okay, well, you've got a phone call. Your sister said I should come and get you. He'll be calling back in twenty minutes."

"Who?"

Straight-faced, Jerry didn't respond.

"Who's calling back, Jerry?"

He turned and shuffled towards the door.

"Aidan."

Erin looked at Spence. "I wonder why he didn't call on my cell phone?"

Spence sat and started shuffling the cards. He didn't react except to say, "Hurry back. I'm winning."

Erin kissed him tenderly. "No you're not." She called out to Jerry, "Hold on. I'm coming."

The beam from Jerry's flashlight lit the path to the farmhouse. Erin walked beside him and wondered aloud, "Did he say what he wanted?"

"Nope. I didn't talk to him. Ben did. Said your cell phone wasn't working."

Erin frowned. Had she forgotten to charge her phone?

How long had it been since she had used it last? In fact, what day was it? Then she remembered blocking calls from Aidan. She hadn't talked to him for at least two months.

"Man, I've been out of it."

Jerry smiled at his young sister-in-law and patted her on the back. "Having fun, are you?"

"More than I deserve, that's for sure."

"Oh, I don't know about that. You've always worked hard. It's time for you to play a little. And after what that ass did, well, who could blame you?"

"Jerry. It's more complicated than that. Spence is my job. I'm supposed to be working here. So far today we've written six words. How am I supposed to explain this to his publisher? She will never hire me again."

"Tell 'em it's a conflict of interest. Tell 'em you've fallen in love."

"Jerry, are you crazy? I'm not in love."

"You got us fooled. I guess you're even fooling yourself. If you're not working, and you're not in love, then what are you doing with that guy? Sorry, honey, from the top of the hill, it looks like love."

Erin bit her lip. Why couldn't she admit that she had fallen in love?

Because he doesn't love me.

She was afraid to think about it. They walked the rest of the way to the farmhouse in silence, Jerry's words a nagging echo.

Ben was standing at the kitchen door, his hand against the telephone receiver.

"Aunt Erin, its Aidan. He sounds mad."

"Thanks, Ben." Erin took the telephone. "Hello? Aidan? What's wrong?"

* * *

"Where have you been? I've been calling your cell phone for months and all I get is your message."

Erin avoided his question. "Aidan, what's wrong? What do you want?"

"Your publisher called. She's been trying to reach you also. Said you're not where you're supposed to be. She has no idea where your client is, either. She's frantic and on the verge of calling the police. I didn't know who else to call. Are you okay?"

"Of course I am, Aidan. I'm fine. I'm sorry, I've been here with the family and I've forgotten to charge my cell phone. I'll plug it in tonight. Don't worry, I'll talk to Patricia. Thanks for calling. Is there anything else?"

"Yeah, now that you mention it. Who's this client she's talking about? And why are you at the farm?"

Erin debated answering him. She glanced around the room, afraid that Ben would hear their conversation. She was alone. Finally, she drew a deep breath and said, "Aidan, it's none of your business. We're not married anymore. Remember? You moved on. Don't you expect me to?"

"That's been over a long time," Aidan said, his voice defeated.

"You mean she left you."

"That makes you happy, doesn't it? Yes, she left me. Go ahead, gloat."

Erin realized she couldn't care less.

"Aidan, I've got to go," she said and hung up. She reflected on the fact that she was able to be flippant and uninterested in Aidan and knew it was because of Spence.

Erin borrowed Jerry's flashlight and headed back to the cabin. Spence was asleep, one of her Jane Austen paperbacks on his stomach. She realized she was still wearing several layers of shirts and pants and sweat beaded on her upper lip. Spence's "eye patch," which counted for one item of clothing, rested on his forehead. He snored softly.

"God, you take my breath away," she whispered.

She went into the bathroom and plugged her cell

phone into a wall socket. The screen lit up. Sixteen missed calls from Patricia and at least two dozen from Aidan. Shoot. She tabbed her way through her address book until she found Patricia McDowell's home phone number. She pressed dial, then put the tiny phone to her ear.

"McDowell. Who's calling?"

"Patricia? It's me, Erin Andersen. I'm sorry to call so late...."

"Why are you whispering?"

"I'm sorry. I've been visiting my family and I don't want to disturb them with this phone call."

"Erin. I'm disappointed. Why haven't you called me before now? And where is Stephen Spence? The man has fallen off the face of the earth. I tell you, I'm about ready to file a missing person report."

"He's with me. Honestly, Patricia, I'm sorry I didn't tell you. I thought it would be best to keep his whereabouts quiet. You see, we couldn't work at his house. I thought that if I could take him away from the familiar, he wouldn't be so distracted. I thought I could keep him under control."

"And how's that working for you?" Patricia asked dryly.

Miserably, Erin admitted it wasn't. "I've never had this problem before. I can't get him to work. Or myself." She giggled hysterically. "It's like we're on this wild vacation and I can't stop."

She ran out of breath. "I can't stop," she repeated.

There was a long silence.

"Patricia? Are you there?"

"Yes, Erin."

Again, silence.

"Say something, Patricia. Yell at me. Shake me out of this dream."

"Erin. Are you telling me that you're sleeping with your client?"

"Yes," she squeaked.

"Have you fallen in love with your client?"

"Yes," she was crying now.

"Erin. This is impossible. I thought that of all the editors I have on retainer that you could handle this job. For God's sake, girl, he's only a man."

"Oh, I know that," Erin moaned.

"Snap out of it," Patricia commanded. "Now you listen to me. You don't stand a chance against someone like him. It's obvious to me now. I thought that you were still heartbroken over that idiot husband of yours. I should have known better. Stephen Spence is handsome and rich, I know. But he's also a playboy. You've seen the magazines. You know what kind of women he dates. Are you one of those women?"

"Yes." Tears slid down Erin's face. "I mean, no."

"It's too late to save this job, but it's not too late to save you. I hold myself personally responsible. I should have seen this coming. Here's what you have to do. Are you listening?"

"Yes." More sniffles.

"Stop crying, girl. Where's your backbone? You need to get out of there right away. You need to get home. I have just the job for you. There's a music teacher–don't worry, he's 86 and toothless. He has the messiest memoirs I've ever read. He's a retired Georgetown professor so he's right across town. You can hop the Metro and work in his stuffy ivory tower. Nothing distracting there."

"But Patricia, what about my deposit?"

"I consider the deposit a wash. I take full responsibility for this. I put you in his clutches, so consider it hazard pay."

Patricia was right. She had been on this fling too long.

"Erin. Are you there?"

"Yes. I'm here. But what about the book?"

"That's not your problem anymore."

Erin didn't notice the shadow moving through the light under the door. "Yes, I know you're right. I should never have done this. I'm sorry that it's ruined our relationship," she said.

"You don't worry about the book. You worry about Erin," Patricia replied. "Like I said, I knew Stephen Spence was trouble and I should never have put you two together."

By the time she hung up, Erin was miserable. She sat on the side of the tub and cried.

"Stupid, stupid. How could I let this happen?" She beat her legs in frustration then jumped at the knock on the door. She locked the door.

"Erin? Baby, are you okay?"

She tore off a handful of tissue paper and blew her nose. "Yes. I'm fine. I'll be out in a minute."

He jiggled the doorknob. "Are you crying?"

"No. I'm going to the bathroom. I'll be right out."

She turned on the shower and pulled off layers of shirts, pants and socks. She stepped in the shower and cried a bit more. Fifteen minutes later she emerged, her skin red, her hair bedraggled. Her eyes were still swollen from crying.

Spence shed a few layers of clothes and sat on the sofa, his arms crossed. He glared at Erin. "So what does Aidan want?"

Confused, Erin hesitated. He thought she was crying because of Aidan? He didn't know it had been Patricia on the phone. She bit her lip, not sure what to say.

"I thought you said that was over."

"I did ...," she trailed off.

"I heard you tell him you were sorry, you shouldn't have done this," Spence said, his face tense. "Just what kind of 'relationship' did you ruin?"

Erin trembled and studied the floor. If she said nothing, it would end and Spence would still write his book. Several heartbeats later he stood and walked to the door.

"It's hot in here. I'm going to sit in the hammock for a

while."

The screen door banged behind him and soon she heard the gentle squeak of the hammock, rocking between the trees.

Erin retreated to the bedroom and pulled out her suitcase. She opened it and began tossing clothes and books in, grabbing handfuls from the bathroom and the living room. Then she started packing Spence's suitcase.

"Are we going somewhere?"

He lounged against the bedroom door.

"Y-y-yes," Erin stuttered. "I have to go home right away."

Spence tilted his head and raised his eyebrows quizzically.

"I can't tell you anymore. I have to go. So do you. You have to finish this book."

"What if I told you I don't care about the book?"

"You don't mean that, Spence."

"What's this about, then?"

Erin knew if she admitted she'd been fired, basically ordered out of his life, Spence would explode. Not that he cared about her, but he would care about the high-handed way Patricia interfered in his life. Then he would break the contract. She used the easiest lie.

"You're right. It's Aidan."

Spence's head whipped up. He didn't expect Erin to admit it. That's why she knew it would work. "He's ... he's in trouble. I have to help him."

"I thought you were divorced. You said he had a girlfriend. Let her take care of him."

"We are divorced, but we still share the same apartment. And she left him."

Spence grinned savagely. "So you're running back, eh? She's gone and the coast is clear. Wait a minute; you still live with him?"

"No. He lives with me. He's been looking for a new place but apartments are hard to find and they're so

155

expensive. I'm not home that often, so I don't even notice him."

"What about his girlfriend? Did you notice her?" His voice dripped with sarcasm.

"I've never met her," Erin admitted. "I know this is upsetting you. I'm upset too. You can keep on writing, though. You'll be so far ahead by the time I get back... ."

"You're not coming back. We both know it."

She turned away.

Spence kicked the living room table, upsetting the lamp. The room fell dark, the light from the bedroom casting shadows. Erin sank to her knees, sobbing. Enraged, Spence yanked her to her feet.

"Why are you doing this to us?"

"I'm sorry." She hid her face in her hands. "I'm so sorry."

His face settled into a stony mask. "You're sorry," he echoed. He grabbed the truck keys off the nail by the front door. "I'm sorry, too. Sorry I met you."

Moments later, the powerful SUV's engine roared to life, its spinning wheels tossing gravel as Spence drove away.

CHAPTER EIGHTEEN

Somber, Erin kissed her sister goodbye, hugged her brother-in-law, patted Ben on the head. She didn't want them to take her to Eaton's tiny airport. She wanted to say her goodbyes then disappear.

A car service had returned the SUV the day after Spence's departure. He chartered a private jet and returned to North Carolina. Instead of driving the large vehicle on the Beltway, Erin turned it in at the car rental counter at the airport, then boarded the small airplane to D.C.

She drew more than a few stares from other travelers. Puffy red eyes and a runny nose made it obvious she'd been crying recently. Four hours and an ear-splitting Metro ride later, she tugged her suitcase up the steps to her Dupont Circle apartment. She put the key in the lock and opened the door. So familiar. Her things were still here, right where she'd left them.

Aidan was in the kitchen cooking. Instrumental music filled the apartment. He was playing her favorite CD. Fresh flowers graced the table. Still, it couldn't comfort her. She ached.

"I'm home," she said, dropping her keys onto the console.

"Hi honey. Rough trip?" Aidan breezed into the living room and kissed her on the cheek. "Here, let me help you." He took the suitcase handle and wheeled it into her bedroom.

"Aidan? Is that you or a doppelganger?"

"Ha, ha. I know you've had a bad time and I want to cheer you up. It's not every day our girl gets fired. In fact, I don't think it's ever happened, has it?"

"Sometimes I wish you were gay. You could have been such a good friend," she said, silently adding "... instead of a lousy husband."

"I can pretend to be gay if it makes you happy."

He pulled into his arms and hugged her.

"I've missed you, Erin," he said, kissing her forehead.

"Aidan. Don't."

"I've made you dinner."

"I see."

"I've got your favorite wine."

"That's nice, but I'm not ..."

"Sshh," he said, putting his finger on her lips. "Just sit and have something to eat."

He pulled out her chair. She didn't think she could eat, but she sat, drained a glass of wine and Aidan served her dinner.

"This is so good. Where did you learn how to make this?" Erin asked, her cheeks stuffed with garlic mashed potatoes.

"Mickey Mantle's. It's a restaurant in New York."

"When did you go to New York?"

"A couple of weeks ago. I got a call from Columbia University. They've accepted me into the post doctoral."

"Aidan! That's wonderful. When can you start?"

"You're not upset?"

"Not at all. I've always wanted you to finish. I've always wanted to call you Dr. Aidan Carter."

"Why don't you go with me? Then I can call you Mrs. Dr. Aidan Carter?"

"Aidan; you don't mean that."

"Yes. I do. I've missed you. No one has ever understood how important my research has been. No one has supported me like you have. You've put up with my idiotic behavior...."

"Is that what they're calling adultery nowadays?" Erin interrupted, gazing into her wineglass.

"Don't say that. I wish I could take back the past two years. I've come to realize how special you are and I don't want to lose you again."

"I'm not yours to lose."

Aidan ignored that. "I know you're tired. I know you're hurt. You need a little rest. Just think about it. Please?"

Erin nodded, too exhausted to finish the argument. She said goodnight and went into her bedroom. Without undressing, she lay on the bed. It hurt to breathe. She touched her lips and thought how they had burned against his. How his hands had touched her, wherever and whenever he wanted. She curled into a ball and cried softly.

The next morning, her door burst open and Aidan bounced into the room. "Good morning sleepyhead."

Erin rolled over grumpily.

"You didn't even get undressed. You should have called me. I could have helped. Here, let me do that."

Aidan pushed her hand away and began unbuttoning her blouse. She caught his hand, stopping him from removing it.

"Aidan. I can't do this."

"Yes you can. I'll help you."

Aidan picked Erin up and carried her into the bathroom. Holding her with one hand, he reached into the shower and turned on the water. Steam began to fill the room.

"That's the nice thing about this apartment. Lots of hot

water. Now get in there," he said, shoving her fully dressed into the shower. He added with a roguish grin, "You want me to wash your back?"

Despite his gentle teasing, Erin's head drooped. She whispered, "I'll never be happy again."

"Yes you will," he said tenderly.

"No, I won't," Erin whispered, as he pulled the bathroom door closed. She leaned against the shower wall so she could cry alone.

* * *

Aidan moved to New York and summer faded. Leaves turned a glorious red and gold before falling to the crowded city streets. Frantic squirrels raced around, creating food caches for winter. Erin moved mechanically through each day, spending her time trying not to think about Spence.

She donated most of her clothes to charity, hoping a new wardrobe would help. She avoided people and kept her cell phone to her ear while she walked the crowded streets or rode the Metro.

The city became gray and dreary. Erin kept busy during the day, conducting research at the library and transcribing notes from the music professor. At night, she pulled on her sweats, crawled into bed with chocolate, and watched old black-and-white movies. She cried occasionally, and it felt good. She gained weight as she settled into her depression.

Patricia soon tired of her angst.

"How long do you intend to mope?"

Erin flinched at Patricia's direct and caustic question.

"I'm not moping." She squirmed in the pin-striped chair, once again. She glanced at the side table and saw the latest issue of the glossy magazine "Them." She caught a glimpse of a sandy beach and a couple walking in the aqua surf. Shuddering, she turned back to Patricia. "I'm fine."

"No you're not. You're moody and fat."

"Sheesh! I'm not fat!"

"Keep it up and you will be. Want a cigarette?" Patricia pulled a pack from her desk drawer and shook it in front of Erin. "Go on; it cuts your appetite."

"No thanks. I'm not interested in getting cancer. You shouldn't be smoking either, you know."

"Eh, I don't. I quit years ago. These are left over,"

Patricia said, examining the crumpled package. "These must be at least three years old."

Erin watched, her mouth agape, as Patricia withdrew a bent cigarette and sniffed it. Her eyes closed and she wore a dreamy smile. "I know it's not fresh, but I can still smell the tobacco."

The older woman slid the cigarettes into her desk drawer and sat back in her leather chair. She templed her thin, bony fingers, stared at Erin and waited.

After several moments of uncomfortable silence, Erin said, "I'm not fat."

"Right. Why don't you give me an update on Professor Campbell?"

With a sigh of relief, Erin bent over and withdrew a folder from her briefcase. She placed it on Patricia's desk. "I've got the last pages of his memoirs transcribed and I'll begin interviewing him next week. I've sent his photo albums to the graphics department for scanning and once they're complete I'll start working on the captions."

Patricia shuffled through the papers. "These are good. Do you think you have enough material for the early years?"

"Too much, actually. He's kept everything. It's the later years that lack depth."

"Humph. Oh well, people want to know about the young and sexy Alex Campbell—the one who slept with all the movie stars going to him for voice lessons. Wasn't Marilyn Monroe his student? It will sell better to younger audiences that way. The only wild-haired old man that sells on book covers is Einstein."

With downcast eyes, Erin agreed. "You're right, of course. I'll concentrate on those interviews," she said, but it was another sexy young man she imagined.

* * *

It was November and she caught the Acela high-speed train to New York. The trip took less than three hours and Aidan met her at the New York Penn Station with a frozen turkey. His bear hug swept her off her feet.

"I hope you know how to cook that," she said, eyeing the bulging grocery sack with mistrust.

He took her hand in his and smiled. "We'll figure it out. I've picked up some things and we'll stop by the deli for a fresh pie."

The trip to New York has been spontaneous. Aidan had called with the invitation for Thanksgiving and, because it hurt too much to think about going home to the farm, Erin agreed.

When Aidan suggested she spend a couple of days in New York, shopping and sight seeing with him, Erin hesitated.

"No hidden agenda; I'll be on my best behavior," he promised.

Erin was glad she accepted his offer and anticipated days of wanton shopping. Thanks to a daily jogging routine, she had shed the extra weight and a few bonus pounds. She joined a local gym and added weight training to her regimen, replacing her soft curves with sculpted shoulders, arms and legs.

She accepted Patricia's compliment with grim satisfaction when the older woman noticed and said, "You're looking much better. Now don't go overboard."

Erin didn't want to admit it, but the older woman's stinging criticism in October had motivated her. Her anger subsided after the first week and then she realized that the exercise and running made her feel good. She also noticed other people jogging in the neighborhood and they nodded to each other. She stopped feeling so lonely.

Aidan hadn't known about her weight gain and subsequent loss, so he didn't notice any physical changes. But he did note the lightness of her step and the confidence in her posture. Tactful, he said nothing.

They caught the green line subway to the Bronx where Aidan had rented a large studio apartment.

"It's only a thousand bucks a month," he said, shoving the door open with his foot, juggling the turkey in one hand and his keys in the other. "I still have some money leftover with the fellowship. It's enough to live on."

Erin stepped inside the short hallway, which led to a small kitchen on the right before opening into a bright and airy room with new hardwood floors. Erin glanced around and noted a bathroom beyond the kitchen. Aidan's large bed dominated the room. Bookcases flanked the walls along with stacking crates filled with clothes. A small, glass-topped bistro table served as Aidan's desk, its surface filled with his laptop computer, folders and papers.

"It's cozy," Erin said, dropping her duffle bag by the bed. "But there's only one bed."

"That's okay, I'll sleep on the floor. Or you can. Or we can sleep together if you promise to keep your hands off of me," he teased, dropping the turkey on the kitchen floor. "It's only for a few days. I couldn't fit the futon in here because of my books. Besides, I don't entertain."

Erin glanced at Aidan, one eyebrow raised.

"Sure, I believe that. Do you realize this is the first time you've had your own place since college? It's strange, isn't it?"

"Yeah, it is strange," he said. "We've known each other for so long. It's lonely, that's for sure." He stepped closer and rubbed a hand up and down her arm briskly. "Oh well. You're here now and we'll have a great time."

Erin tugged her jacket off and tossed it on the bed. She

kicked off her shoes. "Let's get that turkey into the refrigerator and see what's in the pantry."

Aidan laughed. "Funny, ha ha. Like that's going to fit in the refrigerator. And my 'pantry' consists of two cabinets. Things are pretty tight in here."

"I see. We'll make do," Erin said.

* * *

The turkey still had not thawed by early Thursday morning so they headed to Manhattan to watch the Macy's Thanksgiving Day Parade. They shoved their way through the crowd along Central Park West for a glimpse of the bands, balloons and floats. Clowns preceded the parade, flinging confetti and enlivening the crowd.

"Clowns scare me," Aidan said, shuddering. "They're creepy."

Next came the marching bands representing high schools and universities across the United States. Erin couldn't help but smile at the serious expressions on the nervous teen musicians.

Floats filled the street until, hours later, the traditional Rocky and Bullwinkle balloons signified the end of the parade.

The crowd dispersed into Central Park and down side streets. Aidan and Erin worked their way to his favorite restaurant near Central Park South, between the Ritz-Carlton and Park Lane hotels.

"I told you it was great," he said twenty minutes later, sipping a cool draft beer and admiring the baseball memorabilia that decorated the walls of Mickey Mantle's.

After splurging on lunch and a decadent dessert of New York cheesecake, they ambled along Fifth Avenue, admiring shop windows. At Rockefeller Center, they watched people ice skate in front of the giant Christmas tree.

"Thank you, Aidan. This is wonderful," Erin said, her

eyes on an elderly couple holding hands while they skated. "I wasn't looking forward to the holidays but everything is so exciting and all the stores are beautiful here. I'm glad I came."

"I am, too." He turned towards Erin and put a hand on her shoulder. "You know, you can stay if want. Leave D.C. and work here. There's dozens of publishers in Manhattan and you could be a book editor, like you wanted."

Erin bit her bottom lip.

"Thanks, but I like D.C. I'm working on a new project and Patricia and I are getting along much better. I mean, she's forgiven me for the mess I made."

"Are you still seeing that guy?" Aidan refused to call Spence by name.

Erin gripped the railing but kept her focus on the ice skaters. "Oh no, that's been over for months. We haven't spoken since .... There's nothing to talk about."

Several minutes passed in silence.

"Let's go to Radio City Music Hall," Aidan suggested. His spontaneous invitation brought a smile to Erin's trembling lips.

"Sure, that's a great idea. My treat since you bought lunch."

* * *

The turkey finally thawed on Sunday, but by then Erin's trip to New York was winding down. They had spent the days with Erin shopping and exploring Manhattan and in the evenings they went to a Broadway play and a movie. They ate out, and Aidan's small refrigerator filled with leftovers.

Aidan offered the bird to his superintendent and they caught the subway to the Pennsylvania Avenue station. They shared a final dinner at a small Chinese restaurant before walking Erin to the train platform.

"I think this is a misspelling," Aidan said, frowning as

he read his fortune cookie. "Listen to this, 'You will have good luck and overcome many harmships.' That's gotta be 'hardships,' right?"

"Here's mine," Erin said, squinting at the tiny red print. "It says, 'Good luck bestows upon you. You will get what your heart desires.'" She crumbled the slip of paper and tossed it onto her plate.

"Hey, cheer up. We both have good luck fortunes," Aidan said. "At least it didn't say, 'That mole is cancerous.'"

Erin sighed. "It's been wonderful visiting you and going shopping. You've been so nice to me this week. Too nice, actually. You didn't try anything. What's up with that?"

"I promised," Aidan said.

"Yeah, and it was an easy promise to keep. Don't you find me attractive anymore?"

Now it was Aidan's turn to sigh. "Women! You complain if I'm a gentleman, then you complain if I'm not. Make up your mind."

Erin smiled slyly. "You're seeing someone, aren't you? You've moved on. Admit it."

"No, I'm not seeing anyone. There is someone I've been chatting with but it's nothing."

"Chatting? Like online chatting? Are you saying you have an Internet girlfriend? How do you know it's a woman? It could be some hairy shirtless guy with potato chips on his belly, pretending to be a woman," Erin teased.

"Ha, ha, funny. She's a doctoral student in Australia who's also working on climate theory. I know she's a woman because we've had video conferences to share research."

"So, she's Australian?"

"No, she's Japanese. She's studying in Australia."

Erin nodded, not knowing what to say. She searched her heart but couldn't find the jealousy that burned through their marriage and divorce.

"So yes, I guess you could say I'm trying to move on," Aidan added softly.

"That's great. Really, I mean it," Erin said as she glanced at her watch. "Well, it's time for my train. Time to go."

She stood and pushed the chair back. As she reached for her shopping bags, Aidan caught her hand. Standing also, he pulled her close and cradled her head to his chest.

"Erin," he whispered. "You know what you want. Who you want."

She hitched with a sob. Aidan had grown up. She realized, though, not even the tiniest part of her was sad about that. She wondered if she could ever let go of Spence the way Aidan let go of her. "Yes, but he doesn't want me. I ruined it. Nobody wants me now," she wailed.

"Give it time. You're young and beautiful and intelligent ... ."

"Funny how that order is so important to men, instead of intelligent, beautiful and young," she muttered.

"You know what I mean. You're gorgeous and brilliant ..." Aidan trailed off at her glare. "I mean you're brilliant and gorgeous and your fortune today said you would have good luck. Give it some time," he repeated, then kissed her on the cheek and shoved her away.

"Go. Your train is here," he said.

"Thank you. I'll always love you, too. Bye Aidan."

She kissed him hard–on the lips–and smiled wickedly although tears glistened in her lashes. She adjusted her shopping bags and her rolling luggage and walked out of the restaurant.

She stowed her packages in an empty seat and sat next to the window. Leaning her head against the cold plastic pane, she surrendered to the tears.

CHAPTER NINETEEN

I t was mid-December in D.C. and Erin rode the escalator up to the snowy street. The comforting aroma of donuts greeted Metro riders. On one corner, a musician played his saxophone, his case open on the sidewalk to catch coins and dollars. On another corner, a tall man preached loudly, "Whose side are you on?" Handmade signs with black, blocky letters quoted scripture. Another man, this one selling flowers to couples, approached her. "A rose for the lady?" Erin gave him a withering glare, and his hand dropped.

At her apartment entrance, she unlocked her mailbox. Inside she found another letter from Aidan, credit card bills, a magazine and a thick, white envelope. She held it under her nose. Mmmm ... smells expensive, she thought. She slid her fingernail under the flap and tore it open. It was an invitation to a gallery opening in March from her publisher. Enclosed was a return envelope for her R.S.V.P.

For the past several months, at Patricia's insistence, she worked with the 86-year-old musician Alex Campbell and helped him turn in a tidy memoir by deadline. Of course, 86 didn't mean he was dead and often Erin found herself removing his hand from her bottom.

"Dr. Campbell!"

The old man would grimace at her, his best leer. Erin began carrying a ruler and whenever his hands strayed, she smacked them. The device was a familiar one to the old teacher, and he soon developed a fondness for the spunky young woman. He even dedicated his book to her.

"Erin: My glass shall not persuade me I am old, so long as youth and thou are of one date."

"What did you do to that old man?" Patricia asked after reading the inscription.

"I whacked him with a ruler," she replied.

"You should have used it earlier," Patricia said, a sarcastic commentary on Erin's strange affair with Stephen Spence. Erin winced at the cheap shot.

Patricia ignored her pain. "Did you receive our invitation? Did you note that it's formal?"

Erin nodded.

"And will you be attending?"

"Yes. I've already sent my R.S.V.P.," Erin said.

"I'm double checking. You realize it's a gallery opening?"

Erin waved dismissively. "Yes. I'll be there and I'll leave my sweatshirt at home. Do you have anything interesting in the basket? Now that my groping genius is finished, I'm on the market again."

Patricia gave her a large envelope. "Read these queries and let me know what you think. Maybe there is something we'd like to publish."

"Are you asking me to be an acquisitions editor?" Erin felt dazed. Here was a chance to choose her work, to help new writers. There could be an amazing book in this stack of letters.

Patricia smiled fondly. She did care for Erin, despite the Stephen Spence catastrophe.

* * *

"If you're not coming here, then you'll have to spend Christmas in Florida with Mom and Dad."

Erin sighed. "Forget it, Mariah. I'm going to spend a quiet holiday at home."

"Too late; I already called them and they're expecting you. They've even redecorated the spare room. You know, the one Mom keeps filled with fishing tackle and poles."

"You didn't!"

"That's right. They've even bought you a non-refundable plane ticket so you can't worm out. You're going to have to face them sooner or later. I've got to go now. Ben's at the door," Mariah said and hung up.

Enraged, Erin stared at her cell phone. She wanted to fling it against the wall, but she had already lost two phones that way in the past four months.

The small phone vibrated in her hand and she noted the readout: "Mom." She rolled her eyes and punched the green handset icon.

"Yes, Mom?"

* * *

On Christmas Eve, Erin peered out the plane window at the aqua waters of the Gulf of Mexico. Soon she recognized features and spotted glowing green retention ponds, then the moonscape of exhausted phosphate pits. She watched ant-sized cars crawl along I-275. As the plane circled to make a landing, she spotted the Howard Frankland Bridge and shuddered. She wasn't a fan of bridges or tunnels, or airplanes for that matter.

Although her parents lived near Sarasota, the closest large airport was Tampa International. They didn't mind the drive over the Sunshine Skyway but Erin did. She hated the thought of driving on the bridge with the world's longest cable-stayed main span. It frightened her to know that it had replaced an earlier bridge that had been destroyed when a tanker, the "Summit Venture," collided with a pier during a storm. Much of that bridge collapsed into Tampa Bay, taking automobiles and a bus. Thirty-five people died. Only one man survived the fall, when his pickup truck landed on the deck of the "Summit Venture."

It was a horror story that ran through her mind each time she visited. She couldn't hold her breath while crossing the long bridge; instead she panted and gritted her teeth.

"Relax, sweetie," her mom said, reaching into the back seat to pat Erin's arm. "We're almost there."

Erin closed her eyes. The trip to her parent's house was cramped and uncomfortable since her mother sold their car and purchased a pickup truck. "It's easier since my poles fit nicely in the back," she explained. Erin's father smiled. He had always tolerated his wife's life-long obsession with fishing and was compiling a cookbook based upon seafood recipes he created during their 42-year marriage. Without her contributions, he reasoned, the cookbook wouldn't exist.

Riding high in a truck cab meant Erin could see over the sides of the bridge, something she couldn't appreciate.

"Oh my, you should see this," her mother said as she looked through the window. "There are several large sharks following that barge. That reminds me, you should have seen the Mako shark we caught in May. We went out to the fishing grounds and set a few lines. When it hit, I thought it was an amberjack, it fought so hard. Your father had to help me with that one, didn't you Jake?"

He smiled at the memory of shark fin soup and Cajun shark steak.

Erin tried to get her mind off the idea of being on the bridge. "Have you two ever seen a manta ray up close? Well I ...." Erin's voice trailed off at the flood of memories.

"Never saw a manta, but I did hook a ..." her father was cut off mid-sentence with a hand from her mother on his thigh. They shared a glance that said, "Let it go," and rode in silence the rest of the way.

Finally, the truck rolled down the crushed shell driveway that ended at Jake and Beth Andersen's retirement home. The small stucco-covered concrete house had weathered fifty years of Gulf Coast hurricanes and while it wasn't the attractive condo on the golf course that Jake had envisioned, its location on the Intracoastal Waterway meant they could keep their sport fishing boat ready at the dock. The thirty-eight foot vessel cost twice as much as the squat house, but the Andersens were happy. They spent most of their time on the boat, since living north of Sarasota, near Bradenton, gave them easy access to the back bays and the open Gulf of Mexico.

A small dog zipped around the corner of the house and made a beeline for the truck. Yapping and standing on its hind legs, it greeted the Andersens. "Hello baby; come to daddy," Jake said, holding out his arms. The little dog leapt into his arms and licked his face. "That's my girl. Cookie loves her daddy."

Beth Andersen made a face. "Don't let that dog kiss you. I swear, you spoil her rotten."

Once inside, Erin opened the door to the spare bedroom and learned that Mariah had lied: no redecoration had occurred. Fishing poles of all sizes lined one wall and tackle boxes filled with lures and spoons and floats and fishing line crowded the top of the dresser. Old life preservers were piled in one corner while a bait box dominated the other. The room reeked of fish and salt and mildew.

"Gag, Mom! You expect me to sleep in here?"

Bewildered, her mother asked, "Why? What's wrong with it?" She glanced around and saw the bait box. "Oh, that. Don't worry about that. I'll have Jake move it outside."

Erin made her way to the sliding glass doors at the back of the room and slid them open. "Don't you ever lock the house?"

"What for? We're out here on the fringe. I worry more about the boat than the house," her mother replied. "Jake! Come help me clear this room."

The three of them heaved and hauled until the most offensive smelling of the fishing gear was stored on the patio. Erin rummaged for air freshener in the hall closet, then saturated the room with the aroma of lilacs.

Her mother's nose crinkled as she returned with clean sheets. "Ew, what's that smell?"

"Not fish, thank god. Mom, how can you live like this?"

"What are you talking about? Jake and I have a perfectly fine home and a great boat. Now, don't get too comfortable. We have to leave here in twenty minutes to make the Christmas boat parade."

Erin enjoyed the parade more than she realized. Hundreds of small and large boats, power and sail, with twinkling lights and colorful Christmas decorations, circled around the harbor.

Her father relaxed in the captain's chair, a cocktail in his hand and his little dog on his lap. "Pretty, isn't it?"

"Yes, it is pretty," she said. "I'm glad we came."

Her mother stepped out of the cabin. "Honey, where's that bottle of rum? Sorry, Erin, we're out of vodka."

"That's okay, Mom. I don't need anything."

"Well, how about a glass of wine? I've got some crackers and cheese spread, and there are some pretzels in the locker."

Erin smiled as her mother fished, unsuccessfully for once, for party food. Beth could bait a hook faster than she could spread Cheese Whiz on a cracker, and filet a fish more easily than fry an egg. With a husband who fancied himself a chef, why should she care?

"Sure, a glass of wine would be fine."

A couple of hours later both Erin and her father were loopy and laughing. The timid Cookie made her way into

Erin's lap and closed her eyes in content as Erin stroked the dog's ears.

Beth, back at her helm, started the massive diesel engine and turned the bow homeward. She smiled to herself, enjoying the alcohol-induced camaraderie between father and daughter. Jake always knew what to say to the girls, she thought. Her own careless fumbling frustrated her daughters as they moved through puberty and into their teens.

"Boys I understand," Beth thought. As the little sister of four older brothers she had learned to toughen up. Her tomboy ways had barely subsided when she met Jake Andersen in high school. She fell head-over-heels in love with the shy farm boy and, after graduating from school, they married.

She knew her daughter needed to find her own way, however, that didn't mean a little fatherly advice couldn't help.

Jake waited until the giggling stopped.

"Remember when we were crossing the Skyway Bridge today?"

"My eyes were closed the whole time, but yes, I remember."

"Well, that's fine, because I was driving. Your mom is driving now, because I'm too impaired to helm the boat. We're a team that way."

"You're a great team." Erin wondered where this was going.

"Yes we are. But she's just as afraid of bridges as you."

"Really?" Erin never noticed.

Her father took another sip of beer.

"Over time, she grew to trust me to get her across. There are all kinds of dangers out there but if you have someone to help, you can learn to live with them. You become one person after a while."

Erin thought about Spence and how protected she felt with him, even sailing a thousand miles and back. But she would never have what her parents have. Spence was gone forever.

CHAPTER TWENTY

The gallery opening was on the first day of spring–
the vernal equinox. It was a good thing she didn't
have plans, or she would have had to decline
despite Patricia's personal invite.

Not that she had plans lately. Her personal life
consisted of the occasional letter from Aidan and Sunday
morning telephone chats with her sister.

It was boring, but she wasn't complaining. She would
lounge in her nightgown, sip coffee and listen to Mariah
chat about folks at home. About East of Eaton, the new
bookstore in town and about the murder trial of the
surgeon who killed his wife and almost got away. Erin
heard about Tom's mid-term exam woes, Ben's latest
skateboarding accident, and how the baseball team lost its
batting coach when Mike Wolfson returned to the major
leagues. Turns out Alec Boone and Bridget Cormac really
are more than friends, and Mr. Jinks, Sammy's cat, is a
female. In fact, Jinks was a mommy.

"Want a kitten? We've got four and they're climbing
the curtains."

"That's hardly an endorsement."

"Well, they are cute. But darn it, I'm not keeping them.

I don't care what Jerry says."

"Jerry," Erin echoed. "Why does he care?"

"Oh, he says they're great mousers. The truth is he loves the little demons. He'll walk around the farmyard with them clawing their way up his jeans. He has one that he carries around on his shoulder. He thinks they're 'clever' like the talking animals in a 'Peter Rabbit' book."

Erin read Aidan's letters with eagerness. He settled into a loft, spending most of his time reading, having class discussions and researching.

"If you change your mind, you can come live with me," he wrote. "Freelance from here if you like or I can take care of you. I've received a grant from the National Science Foundation and it provides me with housing and a generous stipend."

When she wrote back, her letters were brief and cheery, wishing him well and encouraging him with his research. She ignored his repeated offers.

"I think your latest paper on coastal aquifers and salinity balances was fascinating and I'm thrilled that your laboratory has been funded for another year ...."

Strangely, she found herself anticipating the gala. Being picked up in a limousine and whisked away to a party would be a nice diversion.

She spent Thursday afternoon shopping for the Friday night affair. She settled on a stunning strapless gown by Darius Cordell. Form fitting, the gown ended in a puddle around her feet. The bodice was studded with diamonds. Okay, rhinestones, but at $1,500 they darn well should have been diamonds.

On Friday, she treated herself to a day at the spa, first in a mud bath, then wearing an organic algae mask while one person gave her a manicure and another a pedicure. During the Swedish massage, Erin had a flashback to a summer morning at the lake. A rush of blood flooded her face at the memory and she could swear that she smelled cucumber. She peered across the salon and saw a row of women relaxing on chaises, cucumber slices on their eyelids.

What a waste, she thought, then giggled. It was the first time she had been able to think of him without hurting.

Later than evening, Erin waited in her apartment building doorway for the limo. She was afraid to step out; afraid someone would trample her gown, spill something on the beautiful, faux fur wrap. Her mother's diamond pendants swung from her ears and she clutched her white satin evening bag to her chest.

Abruptly, and with a hail of car horns from irate cab drivers, a long black limousine muscled its way to the curb. The driver, elegant in his tuxedo, stepped out and opened a back door for her.

"Am I the first on your route?" she asked.

"No, ma'am. And I apologize for being tardy."

Erin smiled and, ducking her head, stepped into the luxury sedan.

"Please excuse me," she said turning toward the other passengers. She gaped. There was only one other person in the vehicle and it was Stephen Spence. Devastating and handsome, still tanned in the middle of winter, his teeth flashed in a charming grin. He was more gorgeous than she remembered. She'd never seen him wearing anything fancier than a button-down Tommy Bahama shirt, but tonight he was wearing a black tuxedo, custom-tailored for the event.

"Hello Erin."

She forgot how to breathe. "Hello," she whispered.

She stared ahead, focusing on the ultra-suede seat across from her. Bright tears sparkled in her eyes, threatening to spill. She blinked rapidly. She closed her mouth and breathed through her nose, counting to seven on the inhale, eleven on the exhale. It was a technique for battling anxiety, and the struggle for composure left her trembling.

They rode in silence through the streets of Washington

for several minutes before the limo stopped and another couple clambered into the car. Erin slid next to Spence, making room for the couple, an older, dashing man with a serene woman on his arm. Seeing the empty seat across from the young couple, the husband-and-wife team shifted sides.

"That's better, the man said stretching his shoulders with a sigh. He nodded at Spence and smiled at Erin. "Good evening. I'm George Rockdale and this is my lovely wife, Jane."

He extended his hand in greeting. Spence clasped it and introduced himself. Rockdale turned to Erin. She stammered, and put her hand into his. "It's nice to meet you. I'm Erin Andersen. I'm with the publisher hosting this event."

Mrs. Rockdale smiled graciously at Erin and Spence. "Do you know each other?" she asked.

"Yes."

"No." Erin blushed and stammered. "What I mean is yes, but we haven't seen each other in a long time."

Noting Erin's embarrassment, Mrs. Rockdale changed the subject. "Mr. Spence, what do you do?"

"Ma'am, I'm a lazy, good-for-nothin' sailor. I spend as much time on my boat as I can." His soft, Southern accent hypnotized Erin. She stared at his lips.

He glanced at her, smiling at her sudden fascination with his chin. He rubbed his hand across it, in case he had missed a stray fleck of shaving cream. That, also, fascinated her.

He turned back to Mrs. Rockdale. "I also paint."

"Houses?"

"What?"

"Do you paint houses, Mr. Spence?"

He laughed, his teeth sharp and white. Erin swallowed hard and turned towards the car window. The downtown traffic was light for a Friday. The federal workers had left early in the afternoon, abandoning the city. Its marble monuments and stately buildings were bright in the moon-lit night.

"Well, some folks say I'm an artist, ma'am. I paint on canvas."

"Would you have painted anything I know, Mr. Spence?" Mrs. Rockdale leaned forward in interest.

"Maybe. After tonight, you probably will. You see, this gallery opening is for me."

"How fascinating. You hardly look like an artist. I would have guessed you were a movie star, or a professional athlete. George, don't you agree?"

Mr. Rockdale nodded, admiration in his face.

Erin reeled. Had Patricia told her the art gala was for Spence? No, she was sure of it. Patricia never mentioned Spence or the book anymore.

"Now, all this flattery is beginning to embarrass me. I'm sure Mrs. Andersen here has a much more exciting life, living here in the city and working for a hot shot publisher."

"Miss," she corrected him. "I'm sorry to disappoint you, but my life is simple and would bore you." She smiled at the elderly couple before turning toward her window.

"Now, Miss Andersen, I doubt you're a simple woman. That dress tells me you're not as boring as you claim." Spence smiled.

"You are mistaken. I lead a quiet life."

"A little librarian, eh?" Mr. Rockdale interjected.

"Exactly," Erin agreed.

"Mr. Spence, if you don't mind me asking sir, where are your socks?" Mrs. Rockdale tilted her head towards his feet.

Erin leaned over and looked. Trust Spence to break the rules. He wore black leather deck shoes—but no socks.

"Burned them this afternoon, ma'am," he drawled.

"Whatever for?" Erin couldn't prevent asking.

"Sailor's tradition on the equinox. We salute the first day of spring by burning our socks in a bonfire, and by knocking back a few beers. We don't wear socks again for the rest of the year. That is, until the winter solstice."

Mr. Rockdale chuckled. "It's true, my dear," he said to his wife. "A couple of years ago a friend asked me to join his crew for a yacht race. He called us 'rail meat' because our job was to sit on the windward side of the boat to counteract the heeling. First thing we did before getting onboard was toss our socks in the bonfire. They would only get wet and uncomfortable. I recall there was a lot of beer after the race, too. It's best not to question a sailor's traditions."

The car slid to a stop outside the museum. Ushers stepped to the car and opened the door. Erin and Mrs. Rockdale placed their fingers into gloved hands and slid out of the limo.

Spence appeared at her side and tucked her arm through his. "We'll see you inside. It sure was nice meeting you, Mr. and Mrs. Rockdale."

Instead of following the couple up the marble steps, Spence guided Erin towards an adjoining sculpture garden. She shivered against the frigid air.

"Cold?"

"Yes."

She felt as if she were floating down the steps. Her gown glittered in the dark. They paused in front of a black sculpture, unable to tell what it was in the dark.

"What do you think that is?"

"I already know. It's a thumb," she said.

"Is that right?" He cocked his head. "Well, I'll be. Do you think it was the artist's?"

Erin turned to Spence. Oblivious to the cold, the chilly breeze riffled his wavy hair.

"Spence."

"Erin."

She groped for the right words, but found none.

"You said you'd come back," he said. "You didn't."

She flared. "You left me!"

"No, you left me. I just drove away."

Defiant, Erin lifted her chin and refused to respond.

"How's Aidan?" he asked, his voice tinged with jealousy.

"How's your book?" she countered.

"You first."

She sighed. "Aidan's gone. He's at Columbia University. He has a grant and a long-distance girlfriend. How's your book?"

"I broke the contract and paid back the advance, with interest."

She whirled, her hands outstretched. "Oh no! That wasn't supposed to happen. Patricia told me she had hired someone who would help you!"

"She did. A former drill sergeant. Best drinking and fishing buddy I've had in a long time. Didn't mean he could drag a book out of me. He gave up and he's running a dive boat at the marina. In fact, I think he's seeing my mom."

He turned to her and grinned. "It wasn't the same, Erin. He's not as good a kisser as you are. Turns out he's not as good an editor, either."

Erin hung her head. "Spence. This is my fault. I was supposed to help you, but instead I was selfish. I should have never taken you to the farm. If we had stayed at your house, we would have worked this out. You trusted me and I let you down."

"What are you talking about, Erin?"

"I'm saying I'm sorry I let my infatuation interfere. I let my personal feelings come between me and my job, that I distracted you from working on your book and now you've lost it."

Spence lifted her chin, and slid an arm around her waist. "Erin, how can I convince you that I never wanted to write the book? McDowell dangled a nice boat in front of my nose and I jumped for it. That doesn't mean I want everyone reading my private thoughts. Painting is personal.

It's my secret, and I don't want to share it with the world until it's finished."

Erin bowed her head, her unshed tears glistening at his confession.

"You're the only one I wanted to share it with. The only one I could."

She looked at him then, hope swelling in her chest. A timid smile tugged at the corner of her lips.

He touched her blonde curls. "You've let your hair grow."

"Yes. I couldn't get an appointment with Billy Peachy," she quipped, blinking quickly.

"Still got your sense of humor? You know what else you have?"

"What?" she whispered.

He placed her hands on his heart and kissed her, softly at first. Then, feeling her breasts heave against him, he deepened the pressure.

"Erin, you're so beautiful tonight." He kissed her eyes, her cheeks, moving down to her throat. "Why did you leave me?"

"I'm here now," she said, wrapping her arms around his neck.

He gazed into her eyes. Long, searching moments later, he stepped back.

"Yes, you are. For how long?"

Wounded, she stepped away, her hands curling into fists. "It doesn't matter. Everything's changed."

"I haven't."

"But you don't have your book."

"I never wanted it. I had all I wanted."

Erin's breath caught in her throat and she tried to speak. Did he mean it? Did he mean her? She heard someone on the sidewalk calling for Spence. "You have to go. It's your show."

He held her hand and they walked up the steps to the front of the museum. A worried-looking man, a curator at the gallery, rushed Spence and grabbed his elbow. "Where have you been? We're starting without the guest of honor."

Erin watched as Spence moved away. Bereft, she glanced around. She saw Patricia watching her from across the room. She glided across the floor towards her mentor.

"I see you found him."

"Patricia, why didn't you tell me the gallery opening was for him? Can you imagine how I feel?"

"Would you have come if I had?"

"Maybe. Probably."

Patricia gave her a sidelong look.

"Okay, probably not. I'm falling apart. He still takes my breath away."

"Save it for the romance houses, honey. I'm not in the market for fiction."

"How can you say that? You know I love him."

"Are you through babbling? Yes? Good. If you love him then why did you leave him?"

"What? Are you insane? You fired me!"

"Jobs are a dime a dozen. Why did you listen to me?"

Erin felt betrayed. "Patricia. How can you say that? You're a twisted woman."

"Maybe. What about you and ex-husband? Who divorces a perfectly rotten cheat and then, instead of punishing him forever, lets him live in her apartment? Plays house with the creep?"

"He's gone," Erin whispered. "He's been gone for months."

Patricia pitied the grief she saw in Erin's eyes. "Then what's keeping you from Spence? You say you love him, so why don't you do something about it?"

Erin panicked. "What can I do?"

"What do you want to do?"

Erin grabbed a glass of champagne off a passing tray and downed it in two gulps. "Find him. Keep him. Wish me luck."

"You're going to need more than luck tonight, sweetie," Patricia said, noting the beautiful women crowding the speaker's podium.

Erin stepped away, needing space between herself and the caustic, manipulative woman. She wandered through the crowd, looking for Spence. She recognized many of the paintings from his personal collection and his unfinished canvasses. He's been busy these past few months, she thought. Then she turned a corner and stumbled, aghast. On both sides of the gallery were portraits of her. Spence had finished his "pin up" series. Although each model had different hairstyle and hair color, they all had the same face–hers. Mortified, she looked around to see if anyone recognized her.

"Do you like them?"

Spence came behind her and put his arms around her waist. He rested his chin on her shoulder as he surveyed his paintings.

"Spence! How could you do this to me? What is someone realizes it's me? Oh my God, my boobs aren't that big!"

"You can't imagine how popular they are. I've been offered $60,000 for that one," he said, pointing to the pin up of her in her red dress, lying on the couch. "Remember how much fun we had working on that one?"

There were several she didn't recognize. One featured her from the back, bending over, an icy beer in her hand. In another she wore cut-offs and a red-checked blouse, tied beneath her breasts. She sat on a rock, a fishing pole in her hands. A third featured her with a losing poker hand, naked except for a pair of pink lacy panties. Playing cards shielded the torpedo breasts.

"I didn't pose for those," she said, pointing. "And I never lost a poker game against you."

"I painted those from memory."

"Did you say $60,000? That's crazy!"

"I'd like to think it's because of the artist, but the truth is, I've never had a better model. In fact, some critics say this series could bring back the Pin Up movement."

"Spence. You can't show these to people. I'm practically naked. What if someone sees them?"

"Someone has seen them. I've made the cover of 'Time' this week. Do you live under a rock?"

"I could sue you."

"No need. You can have it all if you want." He squeezed her tight and kissed the back of her neck. "I've missed you, Erin."

CHAPTER TWENTY-ONE

The next morning, Erin peeked out the apartment window. A late, spring snow fell during the night, grid locking the city. Offices closed, traffic stood still.

She picked up a pillow and swatted Spence. "Let's go outside. Make a snowman." She waggled her head toward the winter wonderland to encourage him.

"Mmmmph," he said from under the pillow. "I'm too comfortable."

"Come on. Get up. Let's go outside. I'm getting bedsores. And I want a Krispy Kreme donut. Can't you smell them?"

She tossed up the window and indeed, Spence could smell the donuts baking two blocks away. Erin slid into her jeans, pulled a sweatshirt over her head and struggled into socks and boots. She flexed her feet suggestively and smiled at Spence. "Bet you wish you had socks now," she teased.

"There is a wimp-chill factor," he hedged, slipping his deck shoes on bare feet, "but the wind isn't blowing out there so I'll have to suck it up."

Soon they were dressed, Spence in his tuxedo pants

and white shirt, plus a jacket Aidan left behind. They went outdoors in the cold, crisp morning and walked toward the park. Every few steps, Spence lifted his boat shoe and shook snow from it. When Erin laughed, Spence made a snowball and tossed it, but Erin ducked, and he missed. Her Yankee aim perfect, however, and she hit him in the ear with an icy missile.

At the little park in Dupont Circle, Erin lay in the snow to make an angel. Spence pounced on her and pulled her into his lap, pulling her sweater up to blow raspberries on her cold belly.

"Hey, no fair." She yelped, in between giggles. "Help!"

He retreated after a friendly couple passing by answered her distress call and pelted him with snowballs.

The frenzy escalated and soon dozens of people were in the park tossing snowballs at each other and at slow cars traveling through the circle.

Spence and Erin rolled boulders into a snowman, and Erin offered her scarf for its neck. Spence grabbed her cap and clapped it atop the snowman. Then he grabbed her arms and pulled her mittens off.

"He needs these more than you do," Spence said, shoving the mittens onto sticks and impaling the snowman's sides.

"You wretch. You owe me a new ensemble."

They held hands and walked to a little restaurant down the street. There, they roasted s'mores over a blue flame and drank hot cocoa.

It was a lovely morning and Erin's spirits were revived. Gone were the long, lonely months spent without Spence.

The sun had returned.

They were on the floor of her apartment, reclining on a blanket spread before the fireplace. The warm, woodsy smell intoxicated Erin. Glasses of wine made her head spin. Spence lay beside her, staring at the flames. Erin flipped over to her side and studied his profile.

"Spence."

"Hmmm?"

"I need to tell you something."

He watched the flames.

"Spence. I want you to look at me."

Warily, he turned to Erin.

"It's not bad, Spence. Well, I hope it isn't."

"What is it, babe?" He rolled onto his back, then remembering her request he looked at her.

"I think you should know that I love you."

He snorted.

Horrorstricken, Erin hid her face in her hands.

"No, no, babe. Don't do that. You had me worried, is all. I thought you were going to tell me I had to leave. Don't cover your face. Erin. Listen. I'm glad you love me."

"But you don't love me," came her muffled reply.

"Did I say that? Come here." He pulled her onto his chest, covering her hands with his and resting them on his heart. "So you love me, eh? What do you love about me?"

Erin stuck out her tongue.

"No, I really want to know. Tell me."

"Spence, don't you know how scary it is to say something that important and then you laugh at me? I'm going to cry and you're making fun of me."

Spence cupped her hands and brought them to his lips. Then he kissed her eyes, tasting her tears. "It's okay to be scared, Erin. Now tell me what you love about me."

Erin struggled to sit and Spence let go of her hands. She hugged her knees to her chest.

"I love .... uh."

Spence smiled and waited.

"I love your smile. I feel as if a window opens each time you smile at me," she said.

Emboldened, Erin moved closer to Spence and picked up his hands. She brought them to her face and held them against her cheeks. "Lately, I've been a robot. Walking, talking, working, going about my business automatically. But now you're back and all of a sudden I see everything. I feel everything. Food tastes better. Sex is better. Even my clothes smell better." Erin let go of his hands and lifted the neck of her sweatshirt, inhaling deeply.

"You never say anything negative, and you always say what you mean. You're generous and kind. You want me to go on?"

Spence nodded, crossing his arms behind his head.

"Most of all, I love that you took my arm at the art gallery opening. If you hadn't given me another chance, I wouldn't have been able to tell you that I love you, and that I have, since our first kiss."

Erin's eyes brimmed with tears and she ducked her head. Spence sat and pulled her close, stroking her head and rocking.

"I'm so scared, Spence."

"Why, babe?"

"What if you don't love me?"

He kissed her and she clung, her lips hungry, demanding. He pulled away with some difficulty. "Do you remember that morning at the farm? In the squeaky old bed? We were fooling around and, I don't know what happened, but it all changed. You must have felt it. That's when I knew."

"Knew what?"

"Knew that you loved me, too. Knew that everything had changed. We weren't just messing around anymore. It wasn't just sex. I knew I wanted something more and I could only have it with you."

"More like what?"

"Like you, forever. I love you, too, Erin."

Much later, they lay in bed, filled with a sweet lassitude. Spence's voice broker her reverie.

"Will you come back home with me?"

Erin held her breath, but the need to be sure demanded she ask. "You mean come for a visit? Or give up my apartment?"

"I mean come home again and live with me. I can take care of you. You wouldn't have to work," he said.

She thrilled at the word "home" and felt her stomach flutter. "But I like to work, Spence. I don't need anyone to take care of me."

"Okay. You can work. I don't mind. And you can take care of me."

Erin slipped her fingers into his large, warm hands and squeezed. A tear slid down her nose.

"So it's settled?" he asked. "You'll come home and marry me? Have children with me?"

"Just try to keep me away. I've kept a suitcase packed and in my hall closet ever since that night in the limo when I found out you're a movie star. Or is it a professional athlete? I can't recall."

"Are you ever serious?"

"Always, love."

CHAPTER TWENTY-TWO

Four months later, Erin stood on the pier at the marina in Ocracoke and watched as ex-drill sergeant Mick Smith maneuvered his skiff against the pilings. He tossed her a line and she wrapped it around the cleat.

"Thanks, sweetheart. I've got a dive lesson this afternoon and I need some air," he said as he clunked two diving tanks on the pier.

Erin rubbed her swelling stomach and smiled. Mick caught the gesture.

"When's the wedding?"

"Excuse me?"

He winked. "Well, gal. Appears you're knocked up and I'm asking you, when's the wedding?"

Erin watched a sailboat tacking its way up the sound.

"I'll ask. I'll ask if you're invited, too."

Mick laughed and pulled more empty scuba tanks from the bow of his motor boat. "Well, don't wait too long."

That night, as Spence stroked her belly and kissed it, she told him about Smith's comment.

"He said 'knocked up'"?

"Yes."

"Well, did you tell him that it's up to you?"

"No."

"When will you marry me?"

"As soon as you finish the manuscript."

Spence sighed. "How many pages do we have left?"

"Oh, I think we could wrap it up this week if you promise to focus."

"Baby, it's not my fault. You've been distracting me since we met."

THE END

ABOUT THE AUTHOR

R obin Van Auken is an author with more than a dozen published books, including contemporary adventure, thriller and romance novels.

She and her husband enjoy traveling to the United Kingdom and Europe, and spend much of their time abroad in ruins, castles, cathedrals and museums. She particularly enjoys crypts with mummies, musty libraries and authentic pubs. In the United States, they bounce along the East Coast, traveling from New England to Florida to visit family and friends.

Robin's books include elements of her passions: traveling, boating, scuba diving, hiking, history and archaeology. The characters in her novels have a connection with idyllic Eaton, a fictitious town in Pennsylvania she invented, although many of her books also feature exciting and exotic cities the heroines (and their lovers) visit during the course of their romantic journey.